SINNERS ON FOX STREET

A Novella and Stories

Yolanda Gallardo

T0007283

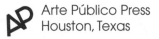

Arte Público Press
Houston, Texas

Sinners on Fox Street is published in part with support from the National Endowment for the Arts and the Alice Kleberg Reynolds Foundation. We are grateful for their support.

Recovering the past, creating the future

Arte Público Press
University of Houston
4902 Gulf Fwy, Bldg 19, Rm 100
Houston, Texas 77204-2004

Cover design by Mora Design
Cover photograph by Joseph B. Raskin

Cataloging-in-Publication (CIP) Data is available.

♾ The paper used in this publication meets the requirements of the American National Standard for Information Sciences—Permanence of Paper for Printed Library Materials, ANSI Z39.48-1984.

22 23 24   4 3 2 1

TABLE OF CONTENTS

WHOSE TRADITION?

Through cold gray eyes, she stands in her habit, staring at the young brown boy reading his composition about tradition. Her breathing is heavy with anger at his words.

"My family likes to celebrate all of the holidays with lots of good food. On Thanksgiving Day, my mother makes a turkey with lots of stuffing. She's a good cook, who likes to cook lots of good food."

Titters spread through the classroom at the loud sigh from the lady with the ruler. "Easter time is lots of fun. We color hard-boiled eggs, and then mommy hides them, and we have to find them. And on Halloween, we dress up in costumes and dunk for apples. That's fun too. I like to dunk my sister's head in the water."

Tap . . . tap . . . tap . . . tap . . . the ruler can be heard hitting the desk over and over again. "And on St. Patrick's Day my mother cooks corn' beef 'n cabbage. I like corn' beef, but I don't like cabbage. It is sour."

BAM! The ruler slams down on the desk, sending shards of wood about the room. The boy's eyes stare in terror as the menacing figure of this mother of mercy grabs the composition out of his hands and tears it to pieces, her hand trembling with fury.

"Those are not your traditions. Those are American traditions. You will stay after school and write a composition that is not based on fiction, young man."

He does not protest. He does not know how. He does not know what he has done wrong. It's the end of the day and the paper before him remains blank.

FOX STREET: A NOVELLA

Prologue

When I first moved to Fox Street, the neighborhood was predominantly Jewish. Everyone knew their neighbors and couldn't help but report everything the children did, which didn't help the situation if you wanted to be bad. Every now and then, we'd suffer a pot of water on our heads for being too raucous in front of the neighbors' windows, but all in all, it was a good place to be brought up, even if it meant the neighborhood women would watch your every move while sitting on their favorite wooden milk crates, knitting, crocheting or just being *yentas*.

Little by little the neighborhood began to change, and, as the moving vans carted away many of our friends, we developed new ones. It changed from a predominantly Jewish neighborhood to Puerto Rican. There were fewer neighbors overseeing us, and we managed to get into trouble with more frequency. It became a different life; some of it is brutal, some of it joyous. I have written *Fox Street* with as much honesty as possible, as much as memory allows. Although I do confess to a bit of embellishment, just to keep your attention.

So, here, with humility and hope, may it serve to stimulate your own memories of the events and environment that account for who you have become.

1

I

Imagine if you will, pouring yourself a tall, cold glass of milk. Then bring that glass to your lips, head back, and let that fresh liquid slide down your throat. Now gulp down that milk with gusto until that tiny piece of wax from the container sticks in your throat. It's just a tiny bit of wax that one more gulp of milk will wash down with no problem. Quickly now, as you are about to wash it down, think of a nice brownish-black roach, any size, with its tiny legs and hard back. Suppose that tiny piece of wax is really not wax but a brown, six-legged . . . now run to the bathroom and vomit your guts out. That's the way we drank milk as kids, and that's the way I still drink milk: vigilant, careful. Milk is supposed to be good for you, right? Sure it is. It's good for your teeth and bones and all kinds of other good things, but on Fox Street you were never sure just what you were eating or drinking, so you didn't take any chances, no matter what they told you in school.

Another thing, did you ever sit down at the kitchen table for breakfast and pour out a bowlful of cornflakes and watch as the roaches hiding in the cornflakes box scattered all over your plate? Did you ever have them crawl over your arms and legs, trying to escape as you brushed them off and stepped all over them? Did you ever feel the squish under your shoes and try to scrape their remains off of your soles, then try to sit down to eat breakfast?

"No, thank you, Mom. I'm going to school."

Now, before you conclude that my mother kept a dirty house, you should know that she had three daughters, me included, and one son and she taught us all to immediately clean up whatever we dirtied. Make no snap judgments. Our tiny four-room apartment was damn clean. My older sister mopped and waxed the floors of that place at least four times a week. And when I say "waxed" I mean you couldn't enter the apartment for over three hours until her floors were dry. What if you had to go to the bathroom? Sound like an exaggeration? Nope! My sister was a housewife since she was five years old. Me, I was more of a tomboy and not exactly immaculate, but I damn right did my cleaning. Or else! "Or else" means getting the shit kicked out of you.

So why the roaches if we were so clean? The whole building was infested. Hell, the whole area was infested. I remember getting up in the middle of the night to go to the kitchen for a glass of water. I opened the door of the cabinet underneath the sink and a mouse scrambled along the top of the door. I ran screaming into the room, waking up my father and mother, who went into the kitchen, me behind them, to kill the mouse. My brother and sisters had all been awakened by my screams as well, and bolted into the kitchen too. There, hanging on the door, was the dead mouse. I had squashed it by slamming the door and didn't even know it.

I don't know why I ran screaming into the room. It wasn't the first mouse I had seen. I had seen rats bigger than cats when some of the kids and I would go swimming in the East River. And how many times had I seen the mice in the house running back and forth from the stove to the sink during dinnertime? It was ridiculous that I would get so upset, but I just never could get used to the vermin.

God, I just thought of the time a friend of mine came to my house for a visit many years later. She had never been in a slum before and to her it was all very exciting. To her way of thinking, we lived fascinating lives, and she couldn't get her fill of stories we told her for hours about our experiences. I guess it's all very colorful and exciting, if you've never had to live it.

At one point in the evening, she went into the bathroom. When she returned, she was white as a sheet. She could hardly talk as she pointed to the floor. My mother and I went in to investigate, and there we saw a squashed mouse. It was half dead, half alive. Apparently, my friend had stepped on it. After embarrassing apologies, as she threw up in the toilet, we quickly swept the half dead mouse into a dustpan, dumped it into the toilet bowl and flushed it away. I don't think my friend ever found the slums fascinating again.

Flushing mice down the toilet bowl always made me nervous. Someone had once told me that a mouse came up out of the toilet and bit her on the ass as she was urinating. I never really believed it, but somewhere in the back of my mind I couldn't forget that story. So I always flushed the chain before sitting on the toilet bowl. Just in case.

Another problem while urinating was the roaches. It was necessary to lift up the toilet cover and seat and shake them, just in case there was anything crawling around the bowl. If you didn't, it was your tough luck if you found a roach crawling on your underwear. Ever try to pee while trying to rip off your underwear? It was no fun, believe me; so you learned to check that bowl first.

As we grew older, we competed with each other trying to kill the rats and mice that ran behind the dressers and under the bed in the middle of the night. We used to take broomsticks and use them as spears. We were like great hunters in the jungle. We'd turn off the lights and wait quietly on our bunk beds, spears ready, until we heard that scratching noise. Someone would switch on the light, and we'd all take aim and, *WHAM,* throw our spears. We killed quite a few of those filthy rodents. Our hunt was often interrupted when my father would come into the room and tell us to go to sleep.

My father used to set up regular mousetraps, the kind that would snap over the mice like a guillotine. I remember a Jewish neighbor, who lived across the hall from us for a short time, had fancy traps. Her traps looked like little cages, and she would call us into her apartment and let us look at the mice she would trap. We asked our mother for those kinds of traps, but she would have no part of it.

None of us ever got bitten by a rat, but one of the kids up the block once had. She was quickly rushed to the hospital and lived, contrary to all the stories we were told. I'm sure a lot of kids died from rat bites but, thank God, I never knew any of them.

I just thought of a clipping in a Latino newspaper that I once saw. It showed a picture of a lady killing a whole bunch of rats in her bathtub. She lived a couple of blocks away. All of us kids just cracked up laughing at the picture. She looked so funny there, holding up a broom in the middle of all those rats.

The worst of all the animals that we had to contend with, in my opinion, were the water bugs. Just in case someone doesn't know what a water bug is, it looks just like a roach but is much larger and much blacker. Those damn giant bugs could fly, or at least it looked like they could. They were much slower than roaches, so they were easier to catch. The problem was, who wanted to catch them? You could hit them with a broom over and over, but they wouldn't die. The only way to kill them was to step on them. Now, who in their right mind wanted to step on those giant roaches? Somebody had to, so everyone would stare at each other and say, "You kill it," "No, you kill it," until the one with the strongest stomach or the one who wanted to appear the bravest would finally step forward and crush it under their shoe, as we all went running away in disgust.

Stepping on a water bug, you could feel the crunch underfoot right up to your teeth. It is the most disgusting feeling I have ever experienced to this day. You just had to vomit afterwards—or, if not immediately after, then sometime during the day.

To tell you the truth, when I found myself alone in the house and one of those bugs would come crawling into the room, I never could step on it. I'd run and get the broom and chase it into one of the holes in the floorboards and hope that the person in the next apartment would be braver than me.

Insects and rodents were just one of the problems growing up on Fox Street. All of the buildings were falling apart. Whenever I think about those buildings, I think about all the housing inspectors and fire inspectors and whatever other kinds of inspectors there were, who were making good salaries somewhere in this city for doing absolutely nothing. My mother always used to say they were going to tear down our building soon and build projects instead. She said that at least fifteen years ago, but that building is still standing today, along with all the others. I did hear some of the other buildings had been condemned, though. I guess the only way those building will come down is when they are burned down.

When my sister and I were still little kids, I remember my mother had put us both in the bathtub for our daily bath. We were having a grand old time. Then as my mother pulled my sister out of the tub and stood her on the toilet bowl to dry her off, *WHAM*, the ceiling caved in right on top of us. That was so frightening, seeing the chunks of plaster come at you. It was sort of like seeing bombs fall in a movie or experiencing an earthquake. We all screamed as my mother grabbed us and took us out of the bathroom to safety. My mother has always been a strong woman, thank God. Otherwise, she would be dead by now, or we would be.

She had told the landlord about the ceiling many times before it caved in, but nothing had ever been done to fix it. Then, it was too late. Then, it was time to sue. My mother took the landlord to court and won. She had a choice between being awarded $1,000 dollars in damages or the building. Wisely, she took the money. The building wasn't even worth that paltry amount, although we kept living there.

Wonder why we didn't move? Maybe because no good neighborhood wanted Latino people moving in, especially not Latino people with kids. Our only choice would have been to move into a similar building in some other part of the city.

Having the ceiling plastered was always a joke to us. The landlord would never hire someone who knew how to plaster. It was too expensive. Instead, he would pay one of the winos around the block a few dollars, and they would do the job badly. They were the same winos we'd see falling down drunk in hallways and on the streets. It was fun for us to watch them plastering as they wove back and forth on their ladders, dropping lumps of wet plaster all over the bathroom tile, which by the way had many tiles missing. It was fun until we had to clean up the mess they left behind.

Anyway, within a year the same ceiling fell in, and again many other times, over and over again. If you were lucky, you would not be under it when it fell. If you were slick, like a lot of people in the building, you'd put plaster in your hair, mess yourself up and scream like hell for one of the neighbors. In those days, the neighbors always came when you screamed. If you weren't lucky, you'd just have to suffer the inconvenience of having a big hole in your ceiling until you could get the landlord to give the wino a few dollars, or until you could finally get somebody from the housing department to force him into it. We always used to argue with my mother when the ceiling fell in. We'd tell her to make believe she had been hurt, but she was too honest for that sort of charade. Besides, she would have felt silly acting.

The one thing I remember most about the landlord was that he never knocked on the door. He always just walked in, catching us in slips or bras and panties as we were getting dressed. My mother used to give him hell every time he made one of his unexpected rude entrances. However, that was about all she could do. And for those of you who are thinking we should have locked the door, think about four kids running in and out of the house all day and try locking up after them each time.

If you're wondering why I've mentioned my mother so many times and my father so few, it's because most of the women around the block were both fathers and mothers to their children. Not that the kids didn't have fathers, most of them did. It's just that fathers had to go out and work all day and, when they came home, they just were not to be bothered with the problems of home, such as raising the kids. They just wanted to come home and find their children in good shape, no bones broken, and it was the mother's job to make sure that was just how he found them.

So Mom became both mother and father to us. With her five-foot-two skinny frame, she fought all of our battles for us with both men and women. She taught us how to survive on that lousy block. We learned things, such as "Don't fight, but if you do fight and you fight with a boy, don't kick him THERE because you can hurt him very badly. But if a man grabs you, yell real loud and kick him very hard THERE and then run, because when he gets up, he'll kill you." And "Don't yell 'help,' yell 'fire;' that way everyone will come running into the hall."

Trying to protect the virginity of three daughters was a very hard job for a woman. Not that she tried to scare us about sex. We had a grandmother to do that. She just didn't want us to turn into whores: *putas*. Sex was something beautiful, not something to be done with just anyone.

One time, a few of the kids around the block and I were looking in the window of a Chinese laundry at a group of men who were playing cards. One of the men stood up, unzipped his pants and pulled out his penis. It was the first time the girls in the group, including myself, had ever seen one. We all screamed, including the boys, and ran away from the window. There was a cop standing on the corner, and we all ran over to tell him what had happened. The girls kept quiet as one of the boys served as our spokesman. This policeman, like many of the other policemen in our area, obviously didn't like Latino kids. With a big smirk on his face, he asked the boy to describe what had happened. The boy just kept saying that the man had pulled out his THING.

"What thing?" The cop kept asking.

The kid didn't want to say the word.

The cop just kept acting ignorant, and kept asking, "What did he pull out of his pants?"

Finally, after exhausting every possibility without saying the word, the kid whispered to the cop, "His dick!"

The cop smiled and asked the boy, "What's a dick?"

All of our faces turned red as the boy screamed out: "His prick! He pulled out his prick."

The cop's face changed expression. "Don't tell me you've never seen a prick before," he said to us, as if he were looking at a bowlful of shit. "You little Spics probably enjoyed it. Now get the hell out of here."

He pushed a couple of us away, and we all ran down the block proclaiming our innocence. When we were far enough away, we called the cop a motherfucker and a bastard and a cocksucker and we all walked along the street mumbling in hopes that his prick would fall off.

A new neighbor moved across the way from us where Elsie, the Jewish lady, used to live. Elsie and my mother had been good friends, and they would talk to each other through their windows as they hung clothes on the clotheslines. They would talk about what a lousy world it was and how someday they were going to move and how they wished they could move to the same neighborhood and re-main friends forever. My mother taught her a few Latino recipes in exchange for matzo ball soup, which was my mother's favorite dish. My mother was friendly with every-one and, as the neighborhood changed, she continued to be-friend those who moved in. Whenever a new Latino family would move around the block, the Jewish neighbors would run to my mother with the news and tell her how awful the situation was becoming. My mother would remind them that we were "Latino" too, and they'd remind my mother that she was different. Next, they'd go into a whole disser-tation on why each of them was wrong. People always did that, no matter what nationality they were knocking. Every group was no good for some reason or other, except for the person in front of them because they were friends. Anyway, most of the Jewish people moved out, including Elsie.

In Elsie's place there came a Latino couple. We very rarely saw the woman of the house. We found out later she was sick. My first vivid recollection of the new neighbors was that of looking out of the window with one of my sisters and seeing the man's nude body as he walked around his apartment. Our windows were only a few feet away from each other, and there he stood, as my grandmother would say, *desnudo en pelotas*, which translated literally to "nude in balls," but which actually means "with everything hang-ing out." That expression is both male and female. My sis-ter and I both screamed and my other sister and brother came to the window to see what we were screaming about.

We were all laughing and screaming hysterically when my mother came into the room and got the full view herself. She grabbed God-knows-what-object from off the television set and flung it across the yard, smashing the man's win-dow.

"What's the matter with you, you pig?" she yelled out to the astonished naked man. "Don't you see there are kids living here?"

After a lot of screaming from my mother and apologizing from the man, he promised to pull down the shades if he was ever to walk around naked again. After that, everything went back to normal.

A few weeks later, I remember the man's wife screaming. My mother, grandmother and a couple of us kids were home when we heard the woman scream. We ran to the window and saw the woman climbing out on the ledge, trying to jump down. My mother called to her, telling her not to jump, trying to find out what was wrong.

"There are two men at my door trying to kill me," she yelled.

My grandmother fell to her knees and begged the woman not to jump, while my mother ran to our kitchen window. From there you could see the hallway of the other building. She yelled at the two men who stood at the woman's door. My mother cut loose, yelling every foul word she could at them, telling them to leave the woman alone.

One of the men walked down to the window of the hall landing and explained, "We're NYPD detectives, ma'am, and we just need to ask the woman a few questions. But it seems she doesn't understand English."

After making the detective show his badge at the window, my mother went back into the living room window and talked to the woman who was still out on the ledge. She explained who they were and what they wanted, that they meant no harm.

Meanwhile, my grandmother was still on her knees praying, and we continued to watch, hoping the woman wouldn't fall or jump. After a while they were able to convince her that she was safe, and she climbed back inside. We never did find out why the detectives were there in the first place, but later that evening her husband called to my mother through the window to thank her for saving his wife's life. He explained that she was very sick with nerves. From then on, whenever my mother hung clothes out on the line, she would talk with the man across the way, just like she had with Elsie.

The last time we ever saw the lady next door—before they took her away—we found out that it wasn't nerves at all but that someone had put some kind of hex on her. It was common in that area to have hexes put on you, and there were many spiritualists that you could go to, to help you out. As more Latinos moved in, more hexes came with them and more *botánicas* (herbs and potions stores) opened.

We found out by accident that the woman had been hexed. We were sitting around the living room watching television, when we saw this bright light come from the apartment across the way. Since we were nosy kids, we all went to check it out and saw a group of people having a prayer meeting around the kitchen table. They had a large candle on the table, and a man stood waving a red cape around it. All of a sudden, the medium, which sat directly in our view, dropped her head to the table. When she lifted it back up, she looked like the devil himself. We screamed and pulled down the venetian blinds because we were scared the devil would see us. Still, we couldn't resist peeking through the slats, our hearts thumping as we watched in awe.

There was a lot of screaming and praying and it looked like the house was on fire every time the man waved his cape. So we kept ducking our heads back in and out and didn't dare look directly into the apartment. Finally, our mother came into the room and discouraged us from looking, with the threat of breaking our heads—*te rompo la cabeza*, a common Latino threat that was never executed.

We sat back down and watched television and tried in vain to peek out through the blinds from our seats.

Most of the parents around the block tried to discourage their kids from believing in hexes and voodoo and evil spirits. Nevertheless, when we'd get together and tell stories of things we had seen, there was no denying that there was some truth to all that business. Every kid would tell a better story than the former one, and after a while we'd scare ourselves so badly that no one would dare walk home. I remember my father coming home at ten o'clock one night and finding a group of my friends in the house, all afraid to leave. He had to walk each and every one of them home, explaining to their parents why they were so late.

Years later when I worked in an office, there was a headline story in the news about a woman who had thrown another woman onto the subway tracks. She had said that she killed the woman because the woman had put a hex on her sister that had made her crippled. All the girls in the office laughed about the idea of witchcraft, except me. All I could think about at the time was a woman I knew when I was a kid, who had been crippled in the same way. I know this may sound crazy, but I saw that woman, who the doctors said had nothing wrong with her, having to be carried back and forth to the bathroom, her legs not able to hold her up. I saw the agony in her face, as she lay helpless in her bed as doctor after doctor and test after test proved that there was absolutely nothing wrong with her. "Psychosomatic" was the word that was thrown around during that time. Maybe that was the problem, but I heard this woman crying many times as she shuffled herself along the living room, her legs trembling beneath her, as she contemplated suicide. I also saw this same woman after meeting with a spiritualist, walking normally one week later after months of being crippled.

I have also seen people of limited learning go into a trance and break out into different languages as if they were their own. I have seen a child of four lay deathly ill in his bed with a high fever and the doctors all saying there was nothing they could find wrong with him. I have seen that same child come walking into the living room and tell his parents not to cry, that his grandpa said everything was okay. When he was asked to describe Grandpa, whom he had never seen and who had died many years before he was born, he did. No fever, no Grandpa. One healthy kid.

I don't want to continue on the subject because I know that many people cannot possibly accept the idea of spirits and voodoo. They were subjects we all knew about living on that block, and most of us believed in them—just another part of our lives, like roaches, rats and falling plaster.

II

There was always something to do but we never seemed to have enough time to do it. Mom used to make us come upstairs by six o'clock, and by eight o'clock it was bedtime. No ifs, no buts. Tuesday, alias Milton Berle day, was the only day we could stay up until nine—only if we were good all day.

We'd all sit around TV watching *Uncle Miltie* dressed up like a girl and laugh like hell when he would yell, "Make up!" If we were bad that day, we were only entitled to see his new outfit, and then we were sent to bed, where we'd strain our ears to hear the rest of the show.

The only other show that we were crazy about was *Howdy Doody*. I clearly remember that "Hey, kids? Do you know what time it is?" And we'd all shout back, "It's Howdy Doody Time." Sometimes, we'd have to yell it from the kitchen table because no one was allowed to watch TV while we were eating. Since we weren't allowed to gulp down our food and we had to eat "like people," meaning civilized people, we'd choke on our food and laughter as we listened to Flubadub and Mr. Bluster. We missed seeing a lot of good squirts of seltzer that Clarabelle would let loose. Mr. Bluster reminded us of a lot of movie stars we would see on TV, and my mother was quick to inform us that it was because many of the movie stars had had facelifts.

Captain Marvel was my all-time favorite comic book character, with "Wonder Woman" taking a close second. I used to love it when Marvel and his whole family would say "shazzam" and everyone would turn into super people. I must have said the "shazzam" at least a thousand times when I was a kid. I was the comic-book-reading champion in my house. I could read ten comics to every one that my older sister read. While she was busy reading one "Lovelorn," I would polish off "Captain Marvel," "Wonder Woman," "Little Lotta," "Richie Rich," "Superman," "Super-Boy", "Superwoman," "Archie," "Elastic Man" and one "Classic Comic," which I hated the most because they always had the lousiest drawings.

My favorite cowboy was Hopalong Cassidy. I loved his hat. I remember crying, begging my parents to please buy me a white horse just like Topper. They would explain to me that it was impossible to own a horse in the city and how there was no place to keep it. Somehow, I never believed that. I swore we could keep it where my father worked, which was in a yard over the bridge. Over the bridge was a place past the railroad tracks not too far away from Fox Street. That area was like the country to most of the kids around there. It had a lot of factories, but it also had trees and was by the East River.

To compensate for not being able to buy me a horse, my parents went all out one Christmas and bought me a complete Hopalong Cassidy outfit. I just kept opening box after box and finding a Hopalong Cassidy shirt, Hopalong Cassidy pants, Hopalong Cassidy boots, Hopalong Cassidy socks, a Hopalong Cassidy jacket, Hopalong Cassidy guns and holsters, a Hopalong Cassidy tie, a Hopalong Cassidy watch, and the outstanding, tall Hopalong Cassidy hat. It was the greatest Christmas I ever had, but only to my mother's dismay, because she just kept hoping I'd finally turn into the little girl she had given birth to. Even she couldn't help but smile, nevertheless. As I strutted around the house in that ridiculous outfit, all three-foot-whatever of me. I was the proudest kid in the world as I walked tall down that filthy street and rounded up all the cattle rustlers I could.

I remember wishing that Hopalong Cassidy was my father and that Doris Day was my mother. I thought Doris Day would make the greatest mother after I saw the movie, *Calamity Jane*. My younger sister always wanted Doris Day for a mother too, but her choice for a father was Jeff Chandler. I don't know whom my brother imagined for his parents, but I do know that my older sister, who wasn't yet a teenager, wanted Frank Sinatra for a husband.

An older cousin of ours took us to see *The Frank Sinatra Show* when it was on television. As we sat there in the audience, a fat lady who sat on one side of me and my sister—sitting on the other side of me—rose, screamed and fainted when Sinatra walked onstage. My sister made me laugh, but the fat lady scared me.

Speaking of idols, none of us could ever understand why my aunt, who used to call me her monkey, would always say William Bendix could put his shoes under her bed anytime.

The movies were something we were always crazy about, especially on Saturday when we would go to the Ace Theatre on Southern Boulevard and see three feature films and twenty-five cartoons. All this for a quarter. Our parents loved it too because we were away from them all day.

My mother would pack us a huge lunch to eat at the movie house and give us each a nickel for candy. We'd always spend the nickel on Sugar Daddies because they lasted the longest. You could lick and lick those damned big brown lollipops until your tongue got sore, wrap whatever was left of it up and save it for the next feature.

Lunch was usually a peanut butter and jelly sandwich, a banana, fried chicken, cookies or any other kind of junk you could fit in the bag. I always loved peanut butter sandwiches, especially the kind they'd give you at school with that stale old bread. Each kid would bring a different assortment of food, and we'd trade bags with each other. My all-time favorite sandwich was an avocado and bean sandwich, which my mother would refuse to make for me. Whenever I would mention how delicious it was, she would cringe at the thought of it and call me a little pig. She would also get very upset when she would catch us sneaking a sugar sandwich or taking a big spoonful of condensed milk. I finally got turned off condensed milk after seeing one roach too many walking on the can.

Anyway, the only thing we all hated was when one of the kids would bring eggs to the movies. They always smelled awful and usually ended up being thrown at the screen or at the fat matron who constantly threw us out of the theatre. We'd always sneak back in through the exit door that one of the kids would open for us.

It was easy for us to sneak into the Ace when we didn't have money. When we wanted to be daring, there was this one wino around the block we used to call "Paladin," because he looked like the character in *Have Gun – Will Travel*. He would always get us in for free when we asked him. He had gotten hold of a badge somehow, so we'd all line up at the ticket taker and march in the theatre pointing behind us until Paladin, who was last, would flash his badge.

One time Clarabelle, from "Howdy Doody Time," came to the Ace theatre to visit all of the kiddies. He was my little sister's favorite, so we took her along. Instead of being happy when he came down the aisle squirting seltzer at us, my little sister screamed bloody murder. She was terrified of her idol, and we had to assure her that he was only playing, trying to remind her at the same time of her love for him.

We didn't always watch the movies that were playing. I don't really think anyone expected us to. We had better things to do, such as rip up the seats, fight with each other, smoke, etc. I had been smoking since I was nine. Everybody who was cool smoked. Nobody at that time was really interested in necking. It was more fun sitting in the adult section and making fun of the couples as they made out. We would watch the men slipping their hands behind the women's backs and undoing their brassieres and we'd roar with laughter until the matron would shine her flashlight in our eyes and sit us back in the children's section. Years later, the Ace became our territory as we fought against the Italian gang. At that time, however, the Ace was just a place to have a good time being bad.

One of the girls in the group had a nasty habit that used to drive us all crazy. There we would be all sitting down quietly in one row, when we'd hear the famous "Uh oh." Everyone would look at each other in horror as she would repeat, "Uh oh." Then we'd all scatter out of our seats, climbing over each other if necessary, as she would pass air. Then we'd all stand in the aisle cursing her as we waited for the air to clear so that we could sit down again and watch the movie.

Sometimes we would actually watch the films that were being shown. That is, we would watch the film until it would break, or it was on upside down, or the voices didn't go with the mouths, or when the actors' voices would begin to gargle. That was our cue for stomping, screaming, whistling, etc.

I remember how happy we all were when we exited the movie house and it was raining, after we had seen *Singing in the Rain*. We danced the whole four blocks home, jumping on and off the curb, stepping gaily in all the puddles with our sneakers. Eight miniature, Latino Gene Kellys.

We were very much impressed with some of the films we saw. I remember seeing *Blackboard Jungle* sixteen times. And then there was some gangster movie that we saw that gave me one of my nicknames: "Ma Barker." My boyfriend at the time was the skinniest, cutest boy on the block, who had long lashes and the largest Adam's apple I had ever seen. He was nicknamed "Machine Gun Kelly." At that time, everyone had a boyfriend or a girlfriend, but the most we would do was kiss.

There was one film in particular, or should I say one scene in a film, that we saw that made a great impression on us. In this scene a man bangs himself against the back of a moving truck, pretending to have been hit by the truck, so he can be nearer his girlfriend, who I think was a nurse. Anyway, when we left the theatre that day, we all kept talking about that scene and then, we finally decided to try it to see if it worked. It did. So that became a game with us. We would all stand on the corner of Beck Street, which was right around the corner from our block, and wait for a car to come down the street. The reason we stood there was that there was a stop sign at that corner and the cars would have to slow down. We didn't want to get ourselves killed.

We would wait there in the shadows for a car to approach, and then, *BAM*, one of us would run out of the shadows and bang our bodies into the back of the car and fall to the ground. The driver would rush out of his car with a stricken expression on his face as the kid played possum. Then the other kids would come out of their hiding places and start yelling at the driver, "You killed him. You killed him." Some of the kids would cry. Everyone would make some kind of a scene while the poor driver would be shaking in his pants. As soon as the driver would turn his eyes away from the (hurt) kid, that kid would jump up and run like a son-of-a-bitch screaming, "Sucker!" Then we'd all split before the driver could gain his composure. None of us wanted to get the shit kicked out of us. Anytime someone says to me that movies don't make an impression on kids, I think of how nice it would have been for them to have been one of the drivers down Beck Street. Come to think of it, though, there were quite a few cars that didn't stop.

I never got hit by a car when I was a kid, except here and there. Once a lady was parking her car and backed up into my leg. All I got was a big cramp out of that bit of carelessness. Another time I was crossing with the light and a car made a turn around the corner. We were both in the right, but I didn't know it. All I knew was "Cross at the Green." Nobody tells you to watch for the turners. I fell down, thank God, and watched the car go over me and stop. The wheels didn't touch me, but as I crawled out from under the car, I couldn't stop shaking or cursing. The driver, who was just as shook up as I was, kept cursing me, and I kept cursing him, and we both kept pointing to the light, him yelling in Spanish and me in English, and that's how it went until he drove away.

The only thing that ever hit me was a bike. It may not seem serious now, but at the time it knocked the wind right out of me, and I couldn't breathe for a few minutes. I kept gasping for air as the street filled up with hundreds of people who watched me convulsing. When I finally caught my breath, someone sat me on the stoop and gave me a glass of water. When I was able to walk, they took me upstairs, and I lay down on the sofa to wait for my mother to come home.

There was one neighbor in particular who used to wait for my mother on the stoop with any disastrous news of the day. Since she was American, we all called her "The Daily News." The Latino *yenta* around the block was called "La Prensa" (that was the Latino newspaper).

"Don't get excited," she would tell my mother. without telling her why. "Don't be nervous. Everything is all right. She's upstairs lying down."

Of course, my poor mother would come running up the stairs, knowing she would find one of her children dead upon entering the apartment.

So there I was, lying on the sofa in all my glory, feeling much better now but waiting for the sympathy due me as my mother entered hysterically, on the verge of a heart attack. When I saw her face, I jumped up fast as a shot and ran around the room, proving to her that all my bones were intact. Then came the screaming and the yelling and the "I told you not to play in the street."

Of course, it wasn't over yet because the same good neighbor would wait for my father, and he'd go through the same changes, but instead of yelling at me, he would yell at my mother, who was supposed to keep the four of us in sight at all times. She did most of the time, even though we lived in the back and our apartment faced the alley. As we got older, she found it more difficult to watch us, and we found it much easier to get into trouble.

Accidents were many with four kids in the house. One time, I was taking care of my brother, who was about eight years old at the time. I had just played a number with my friend Cucho. He wasn't the runner but he promised to put the money on the number for me. A short time later, Cucho came to the house and told me my brother had gotten hit by a car. I thought he was lying and that I had hit the number that he was just kidding around with me. I kept telling him to stop bullshitting, but he kept insisting until I finally believed him. I ran downstairs to find a large crowd hovering around my brother in the street. Someone kept saying, "He went up in the air and came down." I swore he was dead. I couldn't stop shaking or crying as I pushed in through the crowd looking for my brother. People were whispering, "That's his sister" and *"pobrecita"* (poor thing). I was never as happy as I was that minute when I saw him standing up by a car, saying "Please don't tell my mother." He was all right, except that his leg hurt.

The driver of the car that hit him drove us to Lincoln Hospital—which could make a book all by itself—and we waited in Emergency for hours. This was common at Lincoln. The Waiting Room area was always filled with sick, bloody people and so there were no seats available for us. We sat my brother down in a wheelchair and waited.

After about an hour, my older sister came bursting into the emergency room and, seeing my brother seated in a wheelchair, she began to scream hysterically that her brother had been crippled. He of course had to stand up and walk around for her, as I died of embarrassment. After X-Rays, we found out that he was just bruised, and we all went home. We never sued, because the driver was a nice guy who didn't have a license and he was driving someone else's car. Besides, my brother had darted out from behind a truck.

Another time when my father took my mother out for dinner at Alex's Pizzeria, which was over the bridge, before leaving, my mother warned my sister not to use the wringer on the washing machine. But my sister, being the housewife that she was, just had to do laundry and wring out the wash. Standing in the kitchen with her, I was stunned as her hand went through the wringer along with a towel and finally stopped at her elbow. I thought her whole body was going to go through the wringer. Well, she screamed and I screamed and neither of us knew what to do to release her arm. So I had to call Alex's Pizzeria for my parents, and they had to leave their veal cutlet parmesan and rare privacy to untangle my sister.

The same sister had another accident when she had just washed and waxed the floors. I wanted to come inside the house to go to the bathroom. Nobody but nobody was allowed to walk on her waxed floors until they were absolutely dry. That tyrant would actually make my grandmother wait out in the hallway until her floors dried, and that was some accomplishment. That was like a Private telling a General what to do. Well, I begged, I pleaded and then I finally forced my way in and went to the bathroom.

When I came out, we got into our usual argument, which turned into our usual fistfight, and we bashed each other around for a while. No one was home; otherwise, we would have been killed for fighting. Finally, I went into my mother's room and closed the French doors behind me. Funny how all those corroded apartments had French doors. Anyway, my sister charged behind me wanting to continue the exchange of blows, but her arm went through one of the glass panes of the door. When she pulled it out, there blood splattered all over the place. Her arm looked like a whale spouting water. It wouldn't stop bleeding, and she just kept screaming. I grabbed a towel and put it around her arm, as I kept begging her, "Don't tell Mommy." She was too scared to argue, and finally we got our neighbor to take her to the doctor for stitches.

Then, it was my turn. We were going through the same fight for the same reason, except this time she was throwing things at me. I kept ducking behind the bed, avoiding everything she was flinging at me. At one point, I bent down to pick up one of the shoes she had thrown, to throw it back at her, and when I lifted my head, I felt my face crack in two. I had smashed my head into the corner of the dresser drawer right over my eye. I felt the blood pouring down my face, and I swore I was dying. My face felt like it was split in half. I didn't dare look in the mirror. Once again, there was a lot of screaming and "Don't tell Mommy" until I finally made it to the bathroom and put my head under the cold water in the bathtub. When the blood was cleared away, we could see that it was a deep cut over my eye that wouldn't stop bleeding. There were no Band-Aids in the house, so I kept putting toilet paper over the cut. The blood kept coming through. My younger sister was the only one who had a dime to buy Band-Aids but refused to part with it. (I had borrowed a nickel from her and had not paid it back.) After a long argument and a lot of bleeding, she finally agreed to lend it to me on a percentage basis. At that moment, I would have promised her my soul.

By the time my parents came home, all that was left of the battle was the Band-Aid over my eye. Everything was fine, and nobody squealed until later that evening when the blood came oozing down again. My father had to take me to the hospital to have the cut stitched.

I felt much better with my cut tended to, but one mishap led to another. Someone at the hospital stole my beautiful, platinum, religious medallion from me. It was one of my few possessions that I really liked, and I was really angry. And worse, I lost a little respect for my father that day for not making a scene to get my medal back. Unlike my mother, he never was much of a fighter when it came to his kids. Had she taken me to Emergency, I am convinced I would still have my medallion necklace today.

We all had accidents, including the angel who wouldn't lend me the dime to buy a band-aid. She had been playing in an abandoned building when she fell through one of the floors and broke her arm. She knew she would be killed if my mother found out she had been playing there, so she and her friends cooked up a scheme. They all walked over to the P.A.L. (Police Athletic League), a youth center at the corner of Beck and Fox Street, and my little sister, being the actress that she was, threw herself down the front steps of the youth center, pretending to break her arm there. One of the social workers brought her home, and she was taken to the doctor, who put her arm in a cast. We all kept telling my mother to sue the P.A.L., except for my little sister who kept insisting that it was her fault. Years later, she told us what had really happened.

III

Gangs and drugs didn't impress us much while we were in elementary school. Sure, there were gangs in those days, but the members were the older guys, our friends' older brothers or sisters. The newspapers didn't start printing headlines about gangs until years later, when it was our turn.

Drugs meant that your mother and father would kick the shit out of you so bad that you'd end up in the hospital and have no where to come home to when you got out, so they weren't appealing at all. We kept as far away from the junkies as we could. I mean, once in a while, on your way home, you'd run into a junkie shooting up on the stairs, but you'd just squeeze around him and make it into your apartment. I mean, who in their right mind wanted to walk around all bent over, talking with that awful slur. Not us.

I learned how to churn butter in the first grade, and in the second grade they took us to the Bond Bread factory. In the third grade, they made me sew an apron. I hated sewing, and my mother had to come to school for the first time, but not the last, because I refused to sew. Later on, she had to go to school for my younger brother, who didn't want to sew an apron either. In the fourth grade, I lost my voice during a singing contest right in the middle of a song.

When it came back, I spoke just like Julie London, even deeper. Now it's sexy, then it was ridiculous. In the fifth grade, they took us to the Museum of Natural History, where we saw a man petrified in copper. In the sixth grade, I drew a large Santa Claus and won a scholarship for art, which I had to give up after one lesson because I couldn't draw anything but Santa Claus.

Once on the way to school, I saw a lady fall out of an apartment window. She was washing windows and her back was leaning against the window gate, when it snapped and she fell. She was still alive, but it was awful and she was so frightened. I've seen a lot of people die, mostly young people. You can't help but see people die when you live on Fox Street. A lot of people just got used to it, but I never could. Every dead body I saw made me just a little bit sicker, especially when that dead body was one of my friends.

There were so many kids on our block that our mothers tried to get the city to make our street a play street, but the city never would. Each time another kid would get hit by a car, the protesters would come out and, after a futile fight and a lot of petitions, they'd all go back home and just wait, praying that the next victim wouldn't be one of theirs.

We'd open the fire hydrant against our mothers' orders and have a grand old time, lifting the water into an arc with tins cans opened on both ends. Some of the kids who had permission to go into the water would put on their bathing suits. Others, like us, would have to go in completely dressed. Then we'd have to go over to St. Mary's Park when we were through and swing on the swings until we were dry so there would be no trace of our disobeying. Once in a while, Mom would break down and give us permission to get wet, and that was the best time of all. We'd have a ball dragging each other under the water. All we had to worry about was the cops coming or a car barreling down the block.

The cops came to my house a couple of times because someone squealed that I had opened the pump. Once, when my mother was there, I ran inside and hid behind the television set. After Mom had told the cop that I was in Florida and he left, she whipped the hell out of me. Another time, when Mom wasn't home, the cops came to our open fire hydrant and took my father's beautiful new red wrench that he had bought the night before and which I had used. Again, I received a good whipping.

There was one cop—his name was Eddie—who would turn on the hydrant for us. He was a nice guy and everyone respected him. And when he'd tell us to turn off the hydrant, we knew he had a good reason for it, and we did it. There was no bullshit where he was concerned. He was about the only good cop around there.

The other cops would line up all the kids against the wall and search them for the wrench that had opened the hydrant. Sometimes, the really mean bastards would take a couple of the boys over the bridge in their squad car and break their knuckles with their nightsticks.

I remember this one kid who got his ass whipped by a cop while his mother kept screaming for help, trying to pull the cop away. Back then, most people were scared of the police. Most people had a reason to be scared.

My mother wasn't scared of anyone, though. One time, she lit into a cop who was beating some man on the corner for stealing. I think he had stolen a pair of shoes. That cop was just wiping that man out with his club, when my mother jumped in, calling that policeman every filthy word I have ever heard in my life. That cop was furious and was dying to take a swing at her. I was shaking like hell. Maybe it's because she could speak perfect English, or maybe it was that look of defiance in her eyes—I'm not sure—but that cop calmed down fast. She took down his badge number, which I'm sure she didn't do anything with, and we both walked away leaving a very thankful man and a very angry cop behind us. I was the proudest kid on the block.

Cops were always doing something shitty in those days. Like the times when we would stand on the stoop and they would come over to us and line the boys up against the wall and search them. Then, after they would find nothing on anyone, they'd call us Spics and tell us to get our fucking asses home. When we were far enough away, we'd call them lousy micks and wops and then we'd split as fast as hell.

There was one cop in particular who was a real bastard. This creepy cop would scare the hell out of all of us. Some- one once said that he finally got a garbage can thrown on his head from off the roof. I never found out if that was true, but he was mean enough to deserve it. Like the time two girls were fighting, and he drove up. The girls stopped fight- ing and started to run, but he was too quick for one of them. He threw his club at them, and it made contact with a girl's head and knocked her right out on the sidewalk. That's how he did things.

If no one was making any trouble, he would goad us into it. Like when we were playing skellzie. Skellzie was a game of bottle caps that you would try to get into little boxes drawn with chalk. You would snap the bottle cap between your fingers and aim for the boxes. That game could only be played skillfully in the gutter, because there the pavement was smooth. So, anyway, there we were all on our knees, having a good old time, when he drove up and parked his car right on the game. We all moved further down the block and drew another skellzie game with chalk and began to play again. He, of course, drove his car down to where we had moved and parked his car again, right on top of the game. This time we of course protested, and that's all he wanted to hear in order to call us dirty Spics.

Thinking I was tough shit, I muttered, "I'm gonna tell my father!"

He grabbed me so fast that I didn't have time to shake in my pants. "What did you say?"

It was too late to back out now. "I said I'm gonna tell my father!"

This huge smirk came over his face.

But I continued, "If you didn't have a gun, he'd beat you."

Little by little, I became braver as I described my father, who was only five-foot-four, but who I was making into a giant. "He can whip any cop with one hand behind his back!"

Then, miraculously, as I was setting my father up to be murdered, something clicked in the cop's head. He knew my father. My father was the same little guy who paid the cop so he could work on Sundays. Wow! Thank God for graft.

There were good times also. Every week we held a beauty contest in the hallway of one of the buildings. It didn't matter that the stairs were mopped with filthy mops and that the place stunk. There were only two contestants every week. The same two contestants. One of them was my older sister, who was voluptuous for her age, and the other was a skinny little masochist. Every week my sister would walk down the stairs in her bathing suit, and the boys would cheer and whistle. Then the other contestant would come, and the boys would boo and hiss. Every week my sister won her beauty contest, and every week the skinny kid lost. One thing I have to say is that the little masochist was pretty and when she finally blossomed, she must have turned out well—that is, if she ever got over having lost so many beauty contests.

And then there was this nice Jewish lady across the street who would give us that good candy with the fruity stuff inside. She was such a nice old lady who would signal us over to her window with her little finger. We always knew what that meant, and we flew across the street. One of the kids would wash her windows for fifty cents apiece. Mom never let us wash anybody's windows but our own.

Then there was the time I was playing stickball and I swung the bat real hard and hit an old lady in the hair. Mind you, the hair, not the head. She had one of those good, tall hairdos straight from the beauty parlor, and I made a nice thick crease in it so it looked like she had an anvil on her head.

Stickball was always a fun game. I remember my aunt telling us a story about the time she was trying to impress one of the fellas who was playing stickball. She was passing by, pretending not to notice him as she chatted with a friend. Then, *PLOP*, someone landed the ball right in her big mouth. It was jammed in there, and it took a while to get it out. I think her boyfriend was impressed.

There were always delays in the game, mainly because of passing cars, but also when someone would hit the ball up on the roof or into the sewer. Getting the ball from the roof was easy. All we had to do was run up the stairs, but the sewer took a little more time. We'd have to remove the sewer grate, which was heavy, and then lower one of the boys by his feet into the pipes. He would have to mush his hands through the dirty water until he found the ball. Once lowered into the hole, though, there were many treasures you could find, like money, tops and all kinds of good garbage.

Another drag was when the ball would get caught on one of the fire escapes. Sometimes the people who lived in the apartments closest to it would lean out of their windows and throw the ball down to us. Sometimes they wouldn't. Then we would have to boost one of the kids up, and he would have to climb up the fire escape and retrieve the ball.

I remember one time when one of the kids fell off one of the fire escapes as he was trying to work his way up. He landed flat on his back and couldn't catch his breath. We had seen a lot of movies that told you how to take care of the injured, so one of the girls ripped a piece of her slip off and made a bandage to wrap around his head. That was all fine and dandy, except that there was nothing wrong with his head. He had just gotten the air knocked out of him.

It was always rotten when there was nothing you could do, like when some kid got hit by the car and we all stood around and watched him die. A lot of people on Fox Street died waiting for the ambulance to come. We stood there and watched as they drew a big chalk mark around his body and when they had taken him away, we could still see the shape of that kid, marked out in chalk and filled with dried blood.

I remember how all the mothers would come running out of their apartments when they heard a car skid and thump, positive that it was one of their kids that had been hit, and then that final mother would collapse at the sight of her dead child. Everyone would try to console her, but the one thing you could not do was calm down a woman who has just seen her child die in front of her.

There were also those mothers who didn't care. The ones who would leave their kids alone in the apartment while they went out to have a good time with some neighbor or with some man in a bar. There were many of those mothers around the block. A lot of their kids died in fires. I always ask myself why people don't tell their kids to run like hell if a fire starts. I wonder how many kids die trying to put the damned flames out, afraid that mommy's gonna kill them for playing with matches.

I remember how we all stood around the bright red fire trucks and watched the firemen bring out the bodies of little kids in bags. I remember seeing tears in those firemen's eyes as they carried those dead kids out of the buildings, buildings that were firetraps, buildings that had no right to be standing.

But fires and accidents were forgotten as we played tops or marbles and built scooters out of milk boxes and lumber that we would find over the bridge. We'd break up a skate for wheels and we'd paint those scooters all kinds of bright colors with emblems on them. Then we'd play chicken and smash head on into each other, each time earning a few new black and blues for courage.

Courage meant a great deal in those days. Like having the courage to run straight across the subway tracks from the uptown side to the downtown side. The greatest feat of courage was having the balls to run on the tracks from one station to another. Our course was from the Longwood Avenue Station to 149th St. We ran it, scared shitless, but nobody dared chicken out. That was the courage that made you survive through that long war you'd have to fight in order to grow up into an adult.

IV

A man came around the block one day handing out Stevenson buttons, because Stevenson was for the poor and Eisenhower was for the rich. Since we were poor, we pinned on the buttons and yelled, "Boo for Eisenhower." Then we hung a dummy of Eisenhower on one of the lampposts and threw cans and garbage at it. Later on, we burned the dummy and went home to show our parents the free buttons we had been given. A few days later, most of the buttons were in the garbage or lost in toy boxes or swallowed up by the holes in the sofas until no more were left and none of us really cared, because none of us knew who the hell Eisenhower or Stevenson were, anyway.

One day we all burned a big cardboard box in the gutter and danced around it, chanting "We're burning Hitler's house," as we laughed and carried on. Then the German boy who had been playing with us began to cry, and we stopped laughing as he ran into his building across the street. We all felt guilty even though we never knew why.

We all knew how to say "Fuck you" in Chinese. At least that's what one of the older kids told us "Maka Hai Ding Ding" meant. So we all stood in front of the Chinese laundry yelling "Maka Hai Ding Ding, Maka Hai Ding Ding." The owner inside kept shaking his fists at us, and we kept singing the new words we had just learned. We kept it up until the man came running out of his store with a machete and chased us. He chased one of the guys all the way over the bridge and back. He was fast for being so old, so we stopped chanting and found something else to do.

Every kid around the block had talent, at least that's what the talent scout would tell the parents who could afford paying him a dollar a week. I remember how he'd ask a group of us on the street if any of us could sing or dance and how we'd all say, "Not me but so-and-so can." Then he'd go to all the "so-and-sos" houses and tell their parents how he'd heard about their talented children and how important it was to further that talent for just one dollar a week. My older sister used to sing in Ellman's Candy Store all the time for the Jewish people. They'd stand her on the counter, and she'd sing her "I'm Gonna Live till I Die," and everyone would applaud. Ellman would give her a candy bar. Naturally, when the talent scout came around the block, we were the first ones to get hit. Mama enrolled my sister in singing class and both of us in tap and ballet classes.

In tap class, we learned how to brush-brush-step and in ballet class we learned how to move our arms like tree branches. My lessons lasted only a few weeks. My sister went on singing and appeared on Channel Thirteen television along with all the other kids who could afford to continue taking lessons. It was fun watching one of the kids from around the block on TV counting out the one, two, three, four steps with her lips as she tapped, two, three, four. It was more fun watching my sister on TV singing "I'm Gonna Live till I Die" again but this time falling off a ladder into the arms of two boys on the word "Die."

Talent agent or not, there was a lot of talent around the block, and we were always putting on shows to prove it. Most of the time, the money we made went to worthy causes like the "March of Dimes" or the "Jerry Lewis Telethon." Once in a while, we kept the money. Since we lived in railroad apartments, it was easy to divide two of the rooms by a curtain and use one room for the stage and the other for the audience.

One time we all got together and put on a show for coupons. The Catholic Church was collecting coupons for the poor and giving out a prize to the kid who collected the most coupons. I remember how we got a whole bunch of Raleigh coupons and evaporated milk coupons, but the best admission paid was by Rosebud Tolentino, who came in with a few hundred LaRosa coupons. We were a cinch away from winning the prize from the church until Rosebud's mother came looking for her coupons and we had to give most of them back. She let us keep a few.

Anyway, we put on our show, and my older sister sang "I'm Gonna Live till I Die" again, and we all did the tarantella to the song "Lucky Me," banging on tambourines we had bought from the Five and Ten. The same kid tap-danced, still keeping time with her mouth, and I sang "Chattanooga Shoe Shine Boy" as I shined someone's shoes, my face blackened with burnt cork, not really knowing someone might take offense.

Which brings to mind the Halloween when my little brother got dressed up like Aunt Jemima. In those days, nobody bought their costumes in the store. Everybody got made up in mama's old clothes or pop's old suits. We went from building to building collecting candy and money and were having a great old time. Everyone thought the Aunt Jemima costume was the best, until we all knocked on this one door and almost died when a black lady answered. We all got so embarrassed when she looked at my brother, who was rotund in those days, with his kerchief topping his shiny shoe-polished black face. Our embarrassment left as fast as it came when that nice lady let out the heartiest roar of laughter possible and dragged my brother inside her apartment, all of us following. She introduced the miniature Aunt Jemima to all her family, who enjoyed the whole ridiculous spectacle as much as she did. We all thanked them for the candy they gave us as we left their home, but to this day I don't remember any of us dressing up in blackface again, not even the "Chattanooga Shoe Shine Boy."

We collected the most coupons for the church and were awarded a miniature plastic statue of the Virgin Mary that glowed in the dark. It was a letdown, because three of us had handed in the coupons, but there was only one statue and we couldn't divide it between us. All I know is I didn't get to keep it and I never saw it glow.

None of us liked going to church too much, especially so early in the morning, but every Sunday without fail my mother made us get dressed up like it was Easter or something and march us all off to church. She didn't go that often herself, but we didn't question her too much about it, or else. . . . The part I hated the most was having to wear a hat. I always hated hats, especially hats with veils.

My father would give us each a quarter to put in the basket for the poor, but we'd run straight to the candy store and exchange it for pennies. Then when they'd pass around the basket in church, we'd put in a penny each time, which was three times, and we'd end up having twenty-two cents to spend on ourselves.

I never really knew what church was all about. I would always find myself kneeling when everyone was standing and standing when everyone else was kneeling. I finally figured out that it was best to stand in the back of the church with all the other people who didn't know what they were doing. They were always the last to stand or kneel. It was also best standing back there because as soon as it came time for people to get up to receive Communion, it was easier to sneak out.

One of the kids who was just as bad as I was caught on to a gimmick one time. She decided to walk real slow after receiving Communion. She would bow her head down and take what seemed like hours to walk down the aisle of the church until she reached the back. After Mass, a couple of the nuns would go over to her and complimented her holiness, telling her God would appreciate it. We of course were all very jealous because she got so much attention from the sisters. We knew she was just being a hypocrite. So every Sunday that followed, we would all walk very slowly up the aisle, heads bent, holding up the Mass as long as we could. Of course, no one could yell at us because we were just being devout Catholics. We could see out the corners of our eyes how angry the nuns would get, and it was difficult as all hell trying to restrain our laughter.

One kid, who used to go to church with us all the time, had Protestant parents. For some reason, he liked the Catholic religion better. He always took Communion with us and really believed in the whole thing. Years later when he went into the Army and was killed in some stupid accident, we tried to get a priest from our church to speak at his funeral. However, because he had never been baptized, we couldn't get any one of the priests to do the honors. I stopped going to Mass after that. Not that I stopped believing in God, I just stopped believing in priests.

I took piano lessons from an old Latino lady. My parents bought me an old upright piano that my father and his friends delivered. When they were carrying it up the stairs, they dropped it and so it never played right. It didn't matter much, though, because my piano teacher couldn't speak any English, and I couldn't understand Spanish too well. So, I never learned how to play anyway. The only time the piano was used after that was when my uncle would play "Polonaise," the only song he knew, and when my grandmother and her sister would play a Venezuelan waltz on it, which was the only song *they* knew. We used to laugh and call them the "Dolly Sisters" because they would bounce back and forth on that little bench.

Whenever we'd play "Off the Curb," which was nothing more than bouncing a ball off of the curb while the other kids would try to catch it, the ball would end up in this little alleyway across the street. We always ran into the alley to get it until the day they found the father of one of the kids in my class hanging from some pipes in there. No one used to like to get the ball after that, because we were always afraid there would be somebody hanging there or that his ghost would get us.

We were always afraid of ghosts and spirits. One time a little girl had an epileptic attack and was convulsing on the floor of one of the hallways. Someone said that a spirit had entered her body. So, nobody dared touch her, not even the grownups. Finally, one lady picked up the little girl and placed her on the couch in her apartment until her seizure was over. It was our lesson that everything wasn't necessarily spirit related.

There was a big fat boy who lived up the block who used to pay little girls a few pennies to pull down their panties.

Some of the mothers found out about it and threatened his mother with the police if she didn't put him away. The mother of the big fat boy just cried a lot, and eventually they moved out of the neighborhood.

A man tried to attack one of the girls who lived in my building. We were all inside except for my sister, who had gone to confession. When we heard that girl scream, my mother thought it was my sister and she ran into the hallway. The girl ran past my mother as my mother turned and faced the man head on. My mother, you must remember, was small and skinny and she looked something like Gloria Swanson, so I don't know why that man just turned around and ran down the stairs. He could have killed her. Anyway, we all ended up having to go and retrieve my sister from church that evening, each one of us carrying some sort of a weapon—a hammer or a wrench, etc. All of us walked big and bad toward the church as we shook in our pants, positive that the man was still around and that he was going to kill us. As far as that girl who had burst into our home for safety, she was never seen or heard of again, at least not by us.

We used to have a great time throwing water balloons from the roof. One day, one of the older boys was throwing water balloons at us, and somebody threw him off the roof. His body brushed against a lady who was walking up the block. When he hit the sidewalk, he just splatted like a watermelon. After that, we always walked with our heads looking up because we didn't want a body to fall on us.

I almost fell off the roof one day. We were playing Ringolevio—a sort of life-or-death version of tag, originally from New York, which we played on the roofs of our dilapidated apartment buildings—when I miscalculated how many adjoining roofs there were and, instead of jumping over four, I went for five. One of the kids screamed, and I jerked my body back and grabbed onto that ledge with all of my heart and soul. After I was pulled to safety by my buddies and had calmed down sufficiently, we all continued to play the game.

Mom didn't like us to play on the roof, but where else could you get such a great suntan and from where else could you throw a marble over the edge, aiming at a marble that was in the gutter across the street and get fifty marbles back if you hit it? One day one of the kids in the building was taking pictures of her dog Skippy on the roof and Skippy fell off. Well, my brother's nickname was Skippy. When the kids went charging through the hallway yelling "Skippy fell off the roof," my mother almost collapsed. She just kept screaming and shaking, and it took a long while for her to see that my brother was standing right in front of her in the best of health.

After a while almost anything could come flying off the roof. Roberta, my next-door neighbor, just missed getting hit by the picture tube from a television set. A lot of people got hit with flying eggs, but the favorite things to toss from the roof were the sacks of flour and cornmeal that everybody got from welfare.

We never got welfare. Not that we didn't try. After my father lost his job, which he had had for twenty-five years, my mother applied for welfare. Maybe it was because she could speak English so well and because she was a very proud woman who always dressed well that they refused to give it to her. There were a lot of times when there was not too much to eat in the house. Maybe those people from the welfare department wanted her to lose her pride. But when you've had pride all your life, you don't throw it away for a slab of cheese, some canned meat, some sticks of butter and those damned sacks of flour and cornmeal.

I used to go with my uncle's wife to pick up the welfare food for her family once a month. I remember how you'd have to stand in a line for a long time while some city worker would yell at the people in line, treating them all like shit. It used to really bother the hell out of me; just because that clerk wore a suit and was being paid a good salary by the city, he felt superior to all of them.

Anyway, when they'd finally open the doors to the welfare place, everyone would have to present their food tickets inside. As they passed by the counters, the other city workers inside would sneer at them and throw the food on the counter to the people, as if they were pigs or something. I remember wishing that they would all drop dead. The only consolation was knowing that they would all have to die sooner or later, whether they were rich, poor or just the in-between guys who'd threw food at people.

V

One of the P.A.L. (Police Athletic League) teachers had a wooden leg. At least that's what she told us the day she took us all on a trip to Rees Beach. None of us believed her, so we just kept rapping our knuckles against her leg, which felt like flesh to us. She said she couldn't go in the water because she'd warp her leg, and we just kept pinching her leg trying to get her to admit she was lying. The whole time we were there, she refused to change her story. By the end of the day, she went home with a black and blue wooden leg.

After we finished swimming and were getting ready to go home, we were taken to the showers. There we saw all these naked ladies showering, as if they were home in their own bathtub. The P.A.L. teacher kept telling us to take off our bathing suits and shower like everybody else, but we wouldn't get naked in front of strangers for nobody. All the way home on the bus, the boys told us about all the men's things they had seen, and we told them about all the women's things we had seen. We all kept giggling while the teacher kept telling us not to be so silly.

The P.A.L. was a place to have fun back then, not the place where we would discuss our strategy for the next rumble, not until years later. Back then, it was fun playing ping-pong and Chinese checkers and all kinds of games. The best thing about the P.A.L. was that everybody got a T-shirt for free with the famous P.A.L. emblem on it. If you were really lucky, you even got a shiny green jacket to go with it. They were always giving us something, especially on Christmas when they would let us pick out toys and games from a room that was just loaded with good stuff. One thing we could never figure out, though, was where the bicycles and miniature cars went that they'd unload, along with the toys that were supposed to be in that room. I remember how we'd fight our way to be first, just so we could pick up one of those shiny bikes, but first or last, those bikes were never there. None of the big stuff was.

We had a good basketball team that used to play against other P.A.L. teams. Everybody on the team had a pair of shiny green shorts and a jersey with a number on it. We used to think we were great every time we whipped the team from the Catholic school. I remember the first time we ever played against them and how they all would bless themselves before taking a foul shot. We thought that was great, so we all genuflected too before we took any foul shots. After we'd win the game, they'd invite us downstairs and give us all sodas for free. We couldn't believe it. If we had lost, we probably would have fought with them, and here they were being such good sports. We learned from them and started giving out sodas and cookies to everyone we played, win or lose.

We couldn't lose, or so we thought, until that group of black kids from the 21st precinct (it could have been 22nd or 23rd) challenged us. God, any one of those girls was as good as the Knickerbockers and made us look like a bunch of clowns on the court. I used to dread the times we would play against them, especially since our fellas would laugh like hell at us from the sidelines. And it didn't help when our star player would try her famous hook shot from halfway across the court and miss. When she made the famous shot, the crowd would roar, but she only made the shot one out of every fifty tries. We never were good at getting the rebounds.

Then there were the great track meets near Yankee Stadium. They were a *ball*, because there you could win trophies and medals. I mean you felt like a king when they'd hand you a silver, gold or bronze medal, and you'd pin it to your T-shirt and you'd be bursting to get home to show your mother how great you were.

We had arts & crafts classes where we learned how to make puppets out of paper mâché, and baking classes where we learned how to make our very own jelly apples, just like the ones the old man with the wagon sold us on the street for a nickel. I learned how to shoot pool and I learned how to play chess.

We had a short black teacher who taught us how to sing and dance. Tiny as she was, she was tough as nails. Either you did what she said or you were out. If you think Little Miss Two-Time Academy Award Winning Actress Vivian Leigh had trouble with *her* Army officer dance teacher in "Waterloo Bridge," you should have trained with our Miss Kirby.

Nobody crossed her, not even the director of the P.A.L. She kept us all in step, and we swore we could dance. We were a proud group of kids whenever we performed. I remember how she took us all to the Coliseum to perform and how we danced in our black tights and tutus on the platform set up for us. It was a big deal for us, although I have no idea what we represented, unless it was poverty.

I'll never forget the time they hired someone to teach us drama. All the girls, including me, almost died when this tall, handsome blonde man who looked like a movie star came into the room. We all giggled and became shy and embarrassed when this gorgeous man introduced himself as our new drama teacher and asked each of us our names, one at a time. Well, we all broke our asses trying to impress him, doing all the exercises he gave us to the best of our ability. He taught us how to "method act," and we all ducked out of the way of invisible falling cardboard boxes and pianos. We limped across the room like old ladies and then limped across the room like young ladies. We enunciated and did everything he told us, just as if he were God. When the class was over and we were still in the clouds, we walked him to the director's office, where he told the director that he quit. I'll never forget when he said, "None of these kids can even speak English," and walked out. We were all so hurt as he left that building and we prayed that he would drop dead.

We used to like to show off for the P.A.L. teachers. It was fun looking at their shocked faces, especially the ones who came from Long Island or Westchester, as we told them about some of our experiences. They would feel sorry for us. We used to like to get yelled at by them. Some of the kids got no attention at home, so they would purposely be bad just so the P.A.L. teachers would look at them, even if for a moment. One time we went to the store with one of the teachers and as she was buying a pack of cigarettes, we robbed a few cupcakes and Yankee Doodles. When we left the store, we proudly pulled the stolen cakes out of our pockets to show her what great thieves we were. She was furious and refused to speak to any of us, even though we promised her that we would never do it again. Either we returned the cakes and apologize to the owner of the store or she was through with us. She wouldn't budge, not even after we had told her what a thief the store owner was and how he'd write down more in the credit book than what we would buy and cheat our parents all the time. So, after a lot of protesting, we finally all marched back into the store, dying of embarrassment and returned the stolen cakes. We never stole for her again. She was different from some of the teachers who thought it was marvelous how we learned to accept our environment.

The greatest teacher in that place was a big black man with the most fantastic personality in the world. His name was Mr. Thomas, and he was the only teacher that knew exactly what he was doing the whole time he worked there. He was the only one we couldn't con to save our lives, and don't think we didn't try. I mean, he was a good guy that you could confide in and joke with and just have a good time with. But at the same time, if you got out of line, he'd be the first one to throw you out of the P.A.L. for a week, no matter how much he liked you. That man never took sides, not even later when there were many gang fights between the Latino kids, who became the Young Sinners and the black kids who became the Crowns, as each group tried to dominate the P.A.L.

There were many sick teachers who worked there too, such as the one who took us to Bear Mountain on a boat trip. She was *really* sick. I won't forget how scared we were on that boat when it began to rain and there was thunder and lightning. We weren't so much scared of the rain as we were of her as she read us the last chapter in the Bible where it says everyone will die from floods and fire and all kinds of good things. You see, we were scared because, according to her, we didn't have this mark on our head that would save us from destruction. She had the mark, though. An angel had spoken to her and told her she had the mark. We all sat there on that boat in the rain trying to figure out some way to bore holes in our heads to see if we had the mark too.

That same lady had one of her convenient ulcer attacks the day one of the fellas our age confessed his love for her. As she went through her usual pains, which she got whenever we said or did something she didn't like, usually with some added fainting, that boy tried to put a knife through his chest. When they grabbed the knife away from him, she still lay unconscious, and he headed straight for the window. He almost made it out, too. Two of the guys grabbed him as he hung there, until some of the other guys could pull him inside. Those damned ulcer attacks caused a lot of fights between the kids who were sure she was bullshitting and the kids who used to pray around her as she lay down during one of the sets (dances) that we would have in one of the kid's houses.

We'd buy Carbona cleaning liquid and pour it into paper bags on handkerchiefs and sniff ourselves into oblivion. Getting high was just another kick, like the kick we'd get knocking each other out in the bathroom of the P.A.L. You'd take a few deep breaths and then one of the kids would grab you with two fingers on the side of the throat until everything would go black, and down you'd go. This was a big kick until one of the girls went into some kind of seizure and we had to get one of the teachers to get her out of it. We got yelled at, of course, and swore we'd never knock each other out again, but, every so often when we had nothing to do, we'd march into the bathroom and do it again.

School was already a drag, so we had to find things to do with ourselves while we played hooky. When it was warm enough, we would go swimming in the East River. Everybody called it La Playa de los Mojones (Shit Beach) because there was shit and rats and all kinds of garbage floating in it. None of these things really bothered us because the East River was our own private beach. I could never really swim well, so I mainly waded in the water or held on to a rope that was attached to the pier and kicked my feet all around the deep water. Some of the fellas could really swim well and they'd swim all the way to the other side of the river.

Once while I was walking into the water and the water was only up to my waist, I took one step further and went into a deep hole and was completely covered by water. I splashed around but couldn't find any kind of ground under me. I thought for sure I was going to drown and I took one deep breath and threw my body as hard as I could, as far as I could and landed in shallow water again. When I looked around, totally shaken, all the other kids were just swimming away, having a ball. Nobody had even missed me.

Since there were so many factories over the bridge there was always something to rob. The big drag for me was that my father worked around there, so I always had to be careful that neither he nor any of his friends would see me. The easiest place to rob was the sugar cone factory. They used to leave the tins right in front, and we'd all grab a big can of sugar cones and run fast as hell. There was a big bakery back there also and that was always much harder to rob because, if they saw you, they'd chase you, and it was pretty rough running with a bunch of bulky cake boxes in your arms. But we managed and we had some great picnics.

There was a cabin in the woods right near the river, and it became our clubhouse. There we'd roast potatoes and stolen marshmallows and build rafts and catch butterflies and do all kinds of good things. We used to go fishing, but we never caught anything. There was always a case of soda left on one of the Cott trucks behind the soda distributer company at least once a week. At first, we used to think we were robbing the soda, but it finally dawned on us that someone must have left it there for us on purpose, because it was always just one case that was left on that big truck. We never found out who left it for us.

Whenever we needed money, we would break of the locks on basement doors to see what we could scavenge. The best luck we had was when we found a secret entrance to the back of one of the grocery stores. There was no food there, but there were plenty of empty soda bottles, which we took around to the front of the store and cashed in. That went on until the storeowner got wise and sealed off our secret entrance.

Another thing we used to do was keep an eye out for loose change that car owners would leave on their dashboards. We never broke into the cars, just looted them when their doors were unlocked. One time we found the keys in one of the cars and we decided to drive it away. We had never done anything like that before and we were all scared. I knew how to drive because I had driven my father's car up in the country. One time, I even drove it all the way down Bruckner Boulevard, up to Pelham Bay and back. But I was afraid to drive the car we were going to steal. I was afraid the police would get my fingerprints. So, one of the other kids who didn't know how to drive, started the car up with my instructions and we all squeezed in and drove a few blocks. Then we all got chicken, stopped the car and ran out, leaving it parked right in the middle of the street.

I learned a lot about cars and trucks from my father. One time, I even changed a flat tire on a truck for him. I remember how proud he was, showing all the guys who worked with him what a good job I had done on the tire. It was only once in a while that he'd let me work with him in the yard. He wanted me to be a little girl.

I acted like a little girl at times, and I played house, but it was so boring. Who the hell wants to put diapers on dolls and walk around with a baby carriage? And who in their right mind wants to wear a felt skirt with a poodle on it, especially when they could wear a dungaree jacket and dungaree pants instead? Felt skirt and dungarees aside, I did have boyfriends. I got married to the boy with the big Adam's apple. When I say married, I mean we had an elaborate ceremony with bridesmaids and ushers as we walked down the East River pier, which was the aisle, all dressed up in our best clothes. One of the fellas held a Bible in his hands and made us promise to love, cherish and obey each other. We both promised, and then we all went home and changed back into our real clothes and played a good game of kick the can. Neither of us was interested in a honeymoon.

VI

Calling someone around the block a motherfucker was like sealing your death. It didn't matter whose mother you were cursing or whether she was the biggest whore or the nicest old lady, because those words meant you'd better be ready to fight. For example, these two winos were sitting on the stoop arguing over a pint of wine. One of them cursed the other one's mother, and the shit was on. They must have fought for at least a half hour, up the block, down the block, beating on each other in every way possible. No one had ever seen them move that much in all the time we knew them. We thought it was hilarious as they picked up milk boxes and threw them at each other and rolled garbage cans into each other, until the cops came and broke it up.

Maybe it was because we had nobody else in the world except our parents that we loved them so much and forgave them for some of the awful things they did to us. I mean, there were so many times when you wanted to put that knife through your father or burn the whole goddamned house down or just scream bloody murder and throw yourself out a window and end your whole damned ridiculous life altogether.

Maybe it was because deep down inside, somewhere, you knew they really loved you and each other that made it possible for you to forgive them your embarrassment when the cops would come to your house because they were beating on each other. Maybe that's why you could come out of that hole you'd go into when your friends would laugh and tell you how they heard the big fight in your house last night.

There were times, though, that it seemed impossible to forgive, like the time all four of us marched over to the Juvenile Court and begged the people there to put us in a home. You see, to a kid on Fox Street, a juvenile home sounded glorious. That's the one thing no parent could threaten you with. I mean, when your mother would tell you she was going to have you put away, you'd get angry when she wouldn't follow through with her threat. So anyway, after one of the many battles in the house, we all asked the people of the Juvenile Court to put us away, and they just laughed at us and sent us home. When I think about it now, I thank God that the social workers there were as callous as they were, because I dread thinking of what would have become of us had they put us away.

When you're a kid you don't think of why your parents always fight. The only thing you know is that it hurts you. You can't possibly stop to think that, to them, living in those filthy holes that people call apartments is pure hell. Grownups see rats and roaches differently than kids do, especially grownups with kids. Grownups who once were kids with all kinds of ambitions too, just like we had. . . . Grownups who were now heating pots of water on the stove to give their kids a hot bath because the boiler would break down for months at a time. . . . When you're a kid you don't think about how your mother always wanted to be a dancer and your father wanted to go into business for himself and become a millionaire. You never think about how neither of them was able to finish school because they had to go out and work to support their brothers and sisters. You never think that maybe they're fighting because each one blames the other for not being able to get out of the garbage they live in. Nope, when you're a kid, you just blame them for making you miserable and for not moving you to a nice house in the country, like all the schoolbooks talk about.

We were lucky, though, because for every miserable moment we spent in that house there were also good ones. Good ones like watching our parents dance together to hicky Latino records and giggling our heads off. And the time we'd find that quarter under our pillow in place of a tooth. And helping Pop kill the turkey he brought home, while Mom would go running all around the house screaming, cursing him for bringing the damned thing home alive.

It was great hearing Mom sing "Don't Blame Me" as good as Sarah Vaughn could ever sing, while she cooked dinner for us. And when Pop would let us pick out the biggest Christmas tree in the whole lot, and we'd have to saw off the top because it wouldn't fit in the house. And then there was the time that Mom finally let us pick out our own Easter outfits, and my older sister and I finally got straight skirts and we didn't have to wear flair skirts like little kids anymore.

Then there was helping Mom cook *pasteles*, the greatest, most wonderful food in the whole world. I remember how it used to take hours scraping those potatoes and *plátanos* and *yautía* and all kinds of good stuff, sometimes scraping half your finger with them, while she prepared the meat and boiled the eggs and got the olives and the hot stuff ready. We'd all sit around the table watching her as she wrapped up each individual *pastel* in its own little package and put them on to boil. It used to take so damned long for those things to cook, but once they were done and you'd sit there stuffing them down your throat, it was all worth it, especially when you'd get a hot one that made your eyes tear and your nose run.

And there was helping mom paint the kitchen mint green instead of that awful shrimp color that the landlord would make the painters use. We would all do the edges while mom would stand on the kitchen table, painting the ceiling and the walls.

And there was Pop letting you and your friends ride in the back of the truck on the way to Orchard Beach. He'd make sure he hit all the bumps so we would bounce up and down in the back like we were riding in a covered wagon. And there was Mom lining us up in the living room and teaching us how to do the Mambo and the Cha-Cha-Cha, while she'd tell us about how she won the jitterbug contest a long time ago. Mom was real young and always looked like our sister, not like some of the other kids' mothers.

There were all kinds of good times. Like buying a new carpet and all four of us kids carrying it home from the store on our shoulders, with a little help from Mom, of course. And there was rearranging the furniture to go with the carpet. And there were those five-dollar bills Pop would give us to buy Mom a valentine. And there was believing in Santa Claus, even though we'd find big boxes from Macy' s and Alexander's and Gimbels all over our place the week before Christmas.

There were always the big birthday cakes ordered from Valencia Bakery. I remember how we all used to follow the man from Valencia whenever he'd deliver a cake, just so we'd be sure to be invited to the party. And then there was always Mom and Pop's anniversary, when the whole family would visit, and everybody would dance and sing, and we'd entertain them with all our talent. Then our parents would kiss after opening the presents, and we'd all get embarrassed and yell, "Boo" and "Yuck," until Grandma would throw us that dirty look. And then they'd dance to the corny "Anniversary Waltz," and we'd all get sick to our stomachs and run into the room laughing. We were very lucky. Not like some of our friends.

Not like the kid from the next building, who lived with her grandmother because both of her parents were junkies, who eventually died. And there was this kid whose father was a merchant marine and whose mother had to work every day. His brother was a junkie. A lot of my friends' older brothers and sisters were drug addicts, and we were never allowed to go to their houses. And there was this girl whose mother used to make her mop and wax the floors before she was allowed to go to any of the dances. Then when she'd be about to leave, her mother would change her mind and never let her go.

And there was this kid up the block whose brothers were always in jail. And there was this girl who was a lesbian who jumped off the roof. There was a friend of mine whose parents were real strict, who used to change clothes in my house whenever she was going to one of the dances. She ended up pregnant and a junkie. And there was this kid who wanted to be a scientist, whose mother used to bring a different man home to live with them every few months. There were these two boys whose father threw himself onto the subway tracks so that his family could get the insurance, although they never got it anyway. And there was this young girl, whose parents had filthy minds, who ended up taking pills and throwing herself out a window.

Also, there was this kid whose father used to be a numbers runner. The cops were always taking his father away in a patrol car, and he was always back on the street later that evening. One time that kid just broke his whole house apart. I remember that same kid's mother one time chased a girl with a razor blade, because the girl had thrown one of her kids into gushing water from the hydrant.

There were good parents and there were bad parents, but one thing they all had in common was that they all wanted to move out. They would all stand on the stoop talking about how one day they were going to leave the area. Everyone was always talking about moving to Gunn Hill Road, and a lot of people finally did. We used to laugh about that because, if all the people from Fox Street moved to Gunn Hill Road, then Gunn Hill Road would have turned into another Fox Street. The kids were different from the parents. We never talked about moving to Gunn Hill Road. We always talked about running away from home or committing suicide.

Once, when I tried to commit suicide, I drank a whole bottle of iodine and lay down on the sofa to die. I knew that nobody would be home for hours, and that would give me plenty of time to do myself in. Well, I waited and waited and then started to get sick. When I finally got so sick that I couldn't hold it anymore, I went into the bathroom and threw up my guts. I remember that everything kept coming up black, and I was sure that my insides were all black and corroded. I threw up and threw up but didn't die. Maybe it was the ice cream cone I had eaten before swallowing the iodine—I don't know. But I stayed alive, and the only side effects I had was that for a few days everything I ate, I ended up throwing up.

Sometimes we would try to die in groups. We'd all go to the drugstore and each buy a tin of aspirin. There were about twelve aspirins in that little tin, so we'd start popping them in our mouths, taking turns, one aspirin at a time for one, and then it was the next guy's turn. So each of us we would swallow a tin of aspirin, and nothing would happen. Then, we'd go to the drugstore and buy some more. Again, we'd pop them in, and again nothing would happen.

After a second tin each, no one felt much like committing suicide anymore. So we'd think of something else to do.

It was always great when someone would throw away their old linoleum. We used to make "carpet guns" out of pieces of the old linoleum, clothespins and rubber bands. We'd shoot the hell out of each other with them. That was before we learned how to make zip guns, basically a junk gat made up of a barrel, a handle and some sort of firing mechanism. Ours used to sting like mad when you got hit with that tiny piece of flying linoleum. Pea shooters were great too. We'd buy them for a nickel in Joe's Candy Store, which used to be Ellman's Candy store, and then we'd run upstairs and rob beans from the pantry. If Mom didn't have any beans, we'd run into the grocery store, up the corner, scoop up a handful of beans from the big sacks and run like hell.

It was also fun asking Joe, who didn't speak English very well, for Tooty Fruity Ice Cream. We didn't know what Tooty Fruity was at the time but we'd heard someone ask for it in the movies. Joe would go digging into the freezer, looking for this new kind of ice cream that we knew he didn't have and we'd stuff our pockets with all kinds of penny candy. It was easy robbing Joe's candy store until he put up that chicken wire all over the place. Then we had to find another candy store to rob.

There was a Jewish candy store around the corner, but the owners wouldn't even let you get close to the candy. You'd walk in, and the first thing they'd do was ask you how much money you had. Then, they'd pick out the candy for you, which was always worth less than the money you'd give them. Unless you were real quick, they'd shortchange you. If we wanted a soda from the fountain, they'd never let us sit down and drink. We'd have to stand there while the old people would sit on the stools drinking seltzer that they'd buy for two cents. Yuck, seltzer was the worst thing in the world to drink, no matter how thirsty you were.

We hated that candy store more than anything in the world. One time, my little brother went there with a dollar to buy a paint set, and they gave him a girl's make-up kit instead. When he came home, my mother marched right around that corner and told them off. I remember how she told them that my brother wasn't a fairy and how they told her that they didn't have any paint sets and that the make-up kit could work just as well. We all laughed and stuck out our tongues at them when they had to return the dollar. My mother always used to tell us not to buy candy there. Not that she was prejudiced against them because they were Jewish; it was just that those two old people were nothing but a couple of thieves.

I know she wasn't prejudiced because every Sunday, she would send us to the Jewish grocery store to buy cream cheese and bagels. That was our favorite breakfast, and it was better than oatmeal or farina, anytime. I always used to think that Mama was part Jewish because of how much she liked her matzo ball soup and how she'd only let us taste the potato pancakes that our neighbor would give us and hog the rest for herself.

My father liked his rice and beans. That's all he liked. So, whenever it was time to please Pop, we all had to suffer with rice and beans, too. Not that we didn't like the way my mother cooked them. We just didn't like them all the time. Besides, everybody used to say that Spics only ate rice and beans, and we weren't Spics. My mother used to make some good black rice when she'd make black beans. We all liked it until she told us that the rice wasn't black because of bean juice. She used ink-fish (squid). We couldn't believe it. How could she dare give us that without letting us know what it was? We thought we would die and, after refusing to eat that kind of rice anymore, after a few weeks we changed our minds, when we remembered how good it tasted.

Well, as our tastes began to develop, so did we. My sister had already been in junior high school for over a year, and I would be starting soon. So, my mother decided it was time to tell me the facts of life. I thought I knew all there was to know, but she sat me down at the kitchen table and taught me everything that might have been left out of my street learning. And then to make the growing up easier, she gave me my very first brassiere, size 32, double A. I had sworn I was flat chested, and compared to my older sister I was, but somehow that training bra fit me. Embarrassed as I was, I felt kind of proud.

VII

The first time I ever saw a black guy walking down the block with a white girl on his arm, I remember how the whole block started to whisper and laugh at them. There was a whole lot of prejudice against the black people, especially among the grownups. The kids didn't care too much one way or the other, even though we were a little shocked. I remember the girl was so blonde, real blonde, and we weren't used to seeing too many blondes around there, except for bleached ones.

All of our parents were prejudiced in one way or another. Not that you couldn't have friends who were "Colored," as they used to say, but it was so much nicer if you would hang around with the white kids. It wasn't so much black people in general that they were opposed to, because they did the same thing with the Latino kids even though they were Latino themselves. I mean, you could hang around with anyone you wanted to, but when it came to boyfriend time, it was always better to have a boyfriend who was a little lighter than you. I guess it put you one notch up in the world.

Maybe it was because the white people would just assume that if you were a Latino, you were black, and that made our parents so color conscious. Like when they first came off the boat and were forced to live in black areas, because the white people wanted no part of them. Or when they would go to any city agencies and say they were Puerto Rican, and the workers there would just automatically check the box that said Negro on the forms.

My mother once told me that when she went to the hospital to have me, the nurse asked her what her husband's nationality was. When she said Cuban, the nurse just assumed that he was black. It was always a funny story, because after I was born, they gave my mother a black baby and gave me to a black woman. Well, I was very white, and the black woman's baby was very black, and both she and my mother screamed and squawked until they were each given their actual children. I mean, my mother didn't want a black child and that black woman didn't want a white one.

Anyway, there weren't too many nice white Jewish boys around the block, and it was very difficult trying to fill Mama's order for a son-in-law. I remember one time when this big fat Jewish boy had a crush on me. He was awful, and I couldn't stand him. He used to follow me around all the time and drive me crazy. He wore glasses and never cleaned his ears. The other kids used to make fun of me and say that someday we would get married. I got really mad at my mother the time he followed me home, and my mother served him supper and treated him real nice. After he left, she said he was a good boy and would probably become a doctor or lawyer someday.

It was very different the day I brought home a black kid. A lot of my friends were black, and I happened to mention that I liked him for a boyfriend. She treated him nicely too, but there was a funny look on her face the whole time he was there. I was embarrassed for him and hated her for that funny expression. I didn't hate her for too long, though, because when I went to his house his mother gave me that same funny look. He had felt just as uncomfortable as I felt. I remember how he walked me home that day and tried to explain about why his mother didn't want him to go out with a "white" girl. I told him that my mom felt the same way about black kids. We both laughed and thought they were really silly but decided it would be better if we didn't go steady. And we didn't.

Later, during the years when the large slum we lived in became a little ghetto, and every few blocks there was a gang, all sorts of prejudice broke out. Gang territories, gang names and slick jackets and mean rumbles were everywhere. We still had Italians, Irish, black and Latinos as friends and neighbors, but there were new rules to follow. We had to align with the "Young Sinners," "Crowns," "Huns," "Knights" or "Royals," among others. Our friends were still whomever we wanted as friends while everything was neutral, but if, for example, one of our boys got jumped by some of the boys from any other gang, then it was time for war. And in war, there were only two sides: ours and theirs. Not that we stopped being friends; we just cooled it for the duration of the war. After everyone's rights were reestablished and everyone got their pride back, and territories or turfs were again made positive, most of the prejudice went out of the window.

A gang from Prospect Avenue was supposed to be big and bad. I'll never forget how much I wanted to join that gang and walk bad along with them, scaring everyone on the street. When my sister, a friend and I got up the courage to ask them if we could join their gang, we were scared shitless when they told us we'd have to be initiated to prove how tough we were. Well, scared or not, we accepted the challenge. The initiation was simple. Their debs, or the girls in the gang, were supposed to beat the shit out of us, and we were supposed to just stand there and take it. Hell, we weren't crazy, so we asked permission to fight back. I mean, there were about twenty of them and only three of us. They couldn't refuse or that would make them pretty chicken-shit. So they agreed. Well, we stood there on Beck Street, right in front of the P.A.L. and waited for them to charge and kill us.

My sister was a dirty fighter. She was a hair pulling, biting, scratching fighter, and we knew she could take on at least a few of them. My friend and I were used to fighting like boys and we could whip most of the boys around the block. We figured we could take on most of the other girls, without getting killed completely, except for maybe the cap-tain and co-captain who were giants compared to us. Well anyway, they charged and, lucky me with my big mouth, I got the pleasure of taking on the captain and co-captain. Maybe it was because I was the one who suggested we be given the opportunity to fight back that they elected to stomp on my head. Maybe it was because I looked, and was, chicken.

Either way, it didn't matter because they both came running full force at me, ready to kill. I must have had an angel on my side, because when they came charging, I ducked and they both crashed their heads together and went down, neither one of them able to continue fighting. This gave me the opportunity to fight with the smaller girls, the ones my size. In the end, the three of us did all right against them and we were let into the gang.

We felt like giants as we walked with them along 156th Street toward Prospect Avenue, knowing we were just as big and bad as they were. Had my mother known we were going to Prospect Avenue to hang around, she would have whipped our asses, but we were too big-headed about being so tough to worry about that. As we were walking, the leader of the debs picked up a brick and threw it through a car window. Maybe she did it to impress us—I'm not sure— but the three of us just looked at each other unimpressed and kept walking with them. When we got to Prospect Avenue, we met up with the fellas, and we were all introduced as new members. I mean, we really felt like hot shit. We were big time now.

After a while of hanging around and flirting with the boys and doing a whole lot of nothing, everyone began to get bored. The fellas decided on a plan and, because we were still new, we weren't let in on it. We just followed along. I remember how we all piled into this elevator in the only Jewish building left around the area. We weren't sure what they were planning, but when we saw two of the fellas carrying a bucket of paint, we started to get the idea. It was too late to back out as we followed them out of the elevator, and one of the guys knocked on one of the doors. An old man answered and asked who it was. "Spics" was the answer from outside. The old man just kept telling us to go away, but no one in the group was about to leave. Again, they banged on the door. When the man finally opened the door, they pushed him aside and threw the paint all over the rug in his house. Everyone was yelling, "LOUSY JEW! We'll teach you to mess around with Spics!!" I was sick to my stomach as I looked at the paint running all over that rug. Then there was utter confusion as everyone ran back into the elevator and down the stairs, and I found myself running with them.

When we were far enough away, my sister, my friend and I just looked at each other in disgust. Not that we were angels. Hell, we were as bad as the next guy. But we weren't cruel. We didn't hate Jews. We didn't hate anyone.

When we got back together with the rest of the gang, we told them we quit. They called us chicken and told us we couldn't take it. We challenged them angrily, to prove to them that we could take it, but they wanted no part of us. We walked back towards our block, angry and stunned and ashamed of ourselves. We didn't have much to do with that gang again, until the few of them that weren't jailed or dead merged with our new gang a few years later.

Only once living on Fox Street do I remember an actual race war go on for a while. It had nothing to do with gangs. It was just the blacks against the Latinos. It had begun as a fight between two girls outside of the junior high school. A Latina had flicked a cigarette and it landed at the feet of a black girl. The Latina insisted that it was accidental, and the black girl insisted that it wasn't. Each one of the girls had a few of their friends with them and got tougher as the argument became more severe. Whether it was an accident or not, what followed was nothing short of pandemonium.

Both girls agreed to fight it out after school, and everyone sat through the long school hours waiting to see the fight at three o'clock. When three o'clock came and we all piled out of school, what we'd expected to be a two-girl fight turned into an all-out rumble. The black girl's mother and uncle were there waiting for the Latina. In turn, the Latino kids backed up their girl. Some ran home to get their big brothers, and the whole thing began to balloon. The more Latinos that came, the more blacks that showed up, and then after a shove here and there, the whole block broke loose, a pile of people beating the shit out of each other, most of them not knowing why. I found myself getting punched and punching back until I was a part of the whole damned mess, too. Nobody was allowed to be neutral.

After a while, the cops came and broke up the whole thing. One cop carried the Latina into the school. She was unconscious, and everyone stood around watching, spitting out hate. Everyone formed into groups and walked back to their blocks. From then on, nobody would walk to school alone. All the Latinas would walk in groups, and all the black girls did the same. Everyone was suspicious of everyone else, and for a while it seemed that a fight would break out between the Latinos and the blacks any day. The cops were always around the school now, waiting for those outbursts. A lot of the kids, who didn't belong to any gangs, had their parents walking them to school. It took a long time and a lot of beatings before things got back to normal. Things did quiet down and the black and Latino kids who had been friends before went back to being friends. Thank God, because school was bad enough without having to worry about getting there in one piece.

Starting at Junior High School 60 marked a big change in my life. It was an all-girl school, where I found myself living two lives. In school, I made new friends and we'd talk about boys and clothes and make-up and just about any kind of girl talk. Out of school, I was with the guys hitching rides on the back of busses and trucks, making bows and arrows, playing stickball and all sort of things that guys did. I wore my hair in a ponytail, because once you started growing up, if you wore your hair in a boy's bob, you were considered a lesbian. I remember the first time I went to the barber shop, years before, and told them to cut my hair like a boy. My mother almost died when I walked into the house looking more like a son than a daughter. She told the barber later never to cut my hair again unless she gave him permission, which she never did. But now in junior high, everyone wore a ponytail, and so did I.

There were all kinds of new styles to get used to; pink and gray were the only two colors to wear. When singer Pat Boone came out as "The Kid in the White Buck Shoes," we followed suit. None of my group liked Pat Boone, but we loved his bucks. I remember that it was never cool to polish them. Anyone who wore clean white bucks was a square. The only way to polish them was to pat the blackboard erasers on them, letting the chalk fall wherever it wanted to. It was always fun getting a new pair because then everyone would get a chance to step on them until they looked used. The trick was to scrunch up your toes real tight so you wouldn't scream when they stomped on your feet.

Rock 'n' roll came out strong while I was in junior high. There was Frankie Lyman and the Teenagers, the Chantels, the Heartbeats, the Schoolboys and hundreds of other groups. We all used to stand around the stoop harmonizing, we thought, just as good as any one of those groups. We wondered how they had been discovered and hoped that someday some big talent agent would hear us and make us rich and famous too.

We learned how to do the "mashed potato" and the "hop" and the "fish," which eventually became the "grind." I remember the "hop" was a ridiculous dance that had girls' breasts bouncing up and down. One time, my sister and another girl had a contest to see who could make their breasts bounce higher as they danced the "hop."

We used to watch "American Bandstand" on TV and laugh at most of the dancers because we could dance much hipper than they could. We, nevertheless, had our favorite couples on the show, such as "Arlene and Kenny." I always liked it when Arlene would dance with this really skinny boy who looked like my friend with the big Adam's apple. I used to wish she would leave Kenny for him because I was sure she liked him better.

None of us liked "American Bandstand" all that much, though, because there were never any Latino kids on the show. They were all mostly Paddies. We liked the "Alan Freed Show" better. We even went on the Alan Freed show once in a while. It was hard to dance on TV because every time the camera would come near you, you'd get embarrassed and start giggling and telling your partner, "We're on TV. We're on TV." Then you'd die when the camera was on you. After a while, it became obvious that there were favorites on the "Alan Freed Show," too, and while the favorites were dancing, they'd make us stand in the back. One time, my partner was tapping his foot to the music while we were told to stand still. Alan Freed himself came over to us and threw us both off the show. I'll never forget how angry I got.

You had to have special tickets to get on that show. I went and bought red construction paper and printed up counterfeit tickets for every one of my friends on the block. We really screwed them because, if they were expecting a count of fifty kids, they ended up with seventy-five. Like it or not, we were on the Alan Freed show whenever we felt like it . . . that is until they were making everyone exchange their tickets for new ones and one of the jerks I had given a ticket to handed in my counterfeit one. We all got caught and were sent home for good.

I made new friends in junior high, friends that could help you out with any problem you had, friends to exchange clothes with and double date with and talk to on the phone for hours and hours about your secrets, friends that really counted. I'll never forget when my good friend was raped by her stepfather. To a lot of the kids around the block, a "stepfather" was the man your mother would bring to live in the house after your father had split. I remember that my good friend never came back to school after that. One of the girls who lived near her told us that my friend's mother didn't do anything to her lover. She stayed living with him, even after what that bastard had done to her daughter. I remember how we all made plans to wipe that man off the map, but we never did anything, except maybe think about that girl once in a while.

Being a best friend meant shouldering a lot of responsibility. I remember when my friend's father was killed in a car accident. We heard about it when we got to school, and she was absent. The teacher told us what had happened, and we all chipped in to buy a wreath. A few of the girls talked about going to the funeral parlor after school to pay their respects. I remember going with them, but when they went in, I just kept walking around the block. I never had anybody really close to me die, and it was my best friend's father who had died. I walked around that block so many times but couldn't find the courage to go inside until my best friend came outside to get me. Some of the other girls had told her I was outside. I remember feeling miserable, seeing how sad she was and feeling so helpless while she cried, and I cried with her. I just didn't have the strength it took to be a best friend.

I was walking down the school stairs with another best friend, a black girl, when I felt someone behind me give me a shove. I turned around ready to fight and saw that the girl who had pushed me was a big, black girl. She was twice my size. Well, my friend and I continued to ignore the girl behind us, who continued to shove me down a few steps at a time until we reached the ground floor. On that final shove, I finally got brave enough to say, "Tsk." That did it.

"Don't you come clicking your teeth at me, girl," the bully bellowed.

There was no way of chickening out anymore. When I turned to face the big girl, my best friend was gone from my side like a shot. It didn't matter that they were both the same color and that at that time I thought it might help. I was thinking, "See, I got nothing against black people, so there's no need for you to kill me, giant."

My friend wasn't about to get her ass whipped, though. There was no sense in both of us getting killed. It wasn't that I had been pushed to the breaking point that gave me courage. I wouldn't have minded if she pushed me all the way home. It was just that I was cornered, and there was nowhere to go. I took a deep breath, slammed my books down on the floor and got into a position that would have made heavyweight Floyd Patterson tremble.

"Okay man, you wanna fight? Go ahead, man. Let's go, come on . . . I'll wipe your ass all over the place. Come on, man!"

I was ranting like a maniac. I was ready to fight the world. As scared as I was, I must have looked convincing or that angel must have been behind me again, because that giant of a girl just stepped back and refused to fight. I was so glad, I wanted to hug her. Instead, we shook hands and she said I was "cool." I picked up my books and walked proudly out of the school building, and there on the corner stood my friend. When I asked her why she didn't stick around to defend me, she told me that she knew I could take care of that girl by myself. It was hard to resist punching my best friend in the mouth right then and there.

VIII

Some people wore a garrison belt to hold up their pants, like what cops use. Others used it was a weapon and wore one at all times. The trick was to buy one that would fit around your hips like a holster, rather than around your waist. This made it easier for you to snap it off in a second and wrap it securely around your hand and wrist so that it couldn't be pulled away from you. We used to practice daily, ripping the belts away from us as fast as possible, because if you ever got jumped, getting that belt off in a split second was essential. We used to unscrew the different insignias from cars and screw them into our belts, making them as effective as chains, with the added quality of lots of jagged edges that could cut the hell out of someone. We used to practice fighting against each other with them, two by two, sort of like the gladiators.

I'll never forget the time my friend and I were walking out of the P.A.L. and we saw a man beating up a pregnant woman in the middle of the street. He was just punching and kicking her, and she was screaming bloody murder. My friend and I climbed over the little fence that separated the P.A.L. from the street, ripped off our garrison belts and whipped the hell out of that man. We hurt him until he was finally able to get loose and scatter like a rabbit. None of the kids around the block could stand the sight of a man hitting a woman, no matter what his reason was. And this was a pregnant woman, which made it worse. Maybe none of the kids could stand it because too many of them had seen their fathers beating up their mothers, and they couldn't do anything but try to separate them.

Anyway, we walked the woman home as she cried uncontrollably in pain. We asked her if she wanted a doctor, and she said no. Then she told us that the man we had just rescued her from was her husband, whom she loved, but who was a junkie and wanted their rent money to buy drugs. Well, we sympathized with her, although we couldn't understand how anybody could love someone who beat the hell out of them.

After we had made her a cup of coffee and she had calmed down, she begged us to help her find him, because she was afraid for him. She was afraid he might be hurt. We, like the jerks we were, did just that. We went all around the area, checking every bar with her, trying to find her husband. Hell, we were always suckers for anybody in trouble, and this woman did a whole lot of crying. We never did find him, thank God, because if we had, we might have gotten killed. I mean, he was a man and, junkie or not, we were still just two thirteen-year-old girls, no matter how tough we thought we were. After walking around with the woman, who wouldn't stop crying and telling us that maybe we shouldn't have interfered because her poor husband was really a good guy but being a junkie made him crazy, we finally left her and walked home. We were just plain disgusted with the whole thing.

There were a lot of macho men around the block who thought it was great fun to hang out on the street all day, drinking beer and making filthy comments to the women who passed by. These big machos didn't care whether it was a woman passing or a little kid. A female was a female to them, and that's all that seemed to matter. We learned as we got older to ignore the remarks that they'd throw out, no matter how vulgar or obscene. There were times, though, when you just had to turn around and tell them to go fuck their mothers or spit in their faces or whatever. I mean, you could ignore comments like "Look at that fine ass" or "Wow, look at those tits," but it was impossible to ignore things like "I'd give anything to put it between those fine legs and into your cunt." Sometimes, those comments were all said in Spanish and we couldn't understand Spanish too well, but we got the idea, anyway. Our faces would turn red or shed tears of embarrassment and we'd just have to turn around and tell them where to put it.

Most of the time, the macho would just start laughing, joined by his macho friends, while you stood there cursing them with everything you had in your heart. And, once in a while, you'd strike a nerve on one of these filthy creatures, and they'd come at you swinging, ready to beat the shit out of you. That type of macho thought nothing of hitting a woman. I'm not saying that everyone who stood around on the corners would whisper obscenities as you walked by. Some of them were poets who said some very funny things, like "Oh, what sugar! and me with diabetes" or "Oh, what curves! and me with no brakes." But after hearing all the other garbage one time too many, even the cute things made you grit your teeth and spit on the ground.

One thing I never understood was that, if you didn't acknowledge the filthy remarks, the following comment was always "Lesbian." In other words, every woman who walked down Fox Street at one time or another was called a lesbian.

The macho male was not the only type of man who lived on my block. There were plenty of decent men who would never think of saying something filthy to a woman. The macho type was a breed all by itself. The worst ones would stand in groups and yell obscenities to a woman as she walked with her husband or boyfriend. These were really bastards who were just looking for a fight, knowing that with guys behind them, they couldn't lose. It was up to the husband or boyfriend to either challenge the macho, which meant getting a beating or maybe even killed, or to ignore him completely.

Becoming a woman on Fox Street meant learning to dig your fingernails into your boyfriend's arm, whenever a remark was made, letting him know that you didn't want him to, or expect him to, retaliate. Becoming a woman was letting him know that you knew he was a man and that he could protect you without letting himself get killed for your honor.

Getting flipped (someone grabbing your ass) was another favorite of the same animal. The flipping kind was almost always with a group, because it was a sure thing that you would turn around and start swinging. There were times when a woman could get away with slapping one of these machos, but there were times when a macho would slap or even punch back. Again, garrison belts came in very handy.

One time, my friend and I were walking home from the P.A.L., when we passed a group of machos hanging around the front of a store. One of them grabbed my friend's ass, and she turned and punched him so hard that she broke a few of his teeth, and he fell flat to the ground. He yelled through his bloody mouth for his friends to jump us. As they came at us, we whipped off our garrison belts, wrapped them securely around our wrists and stood ready to kill. His pals stopped short when they saw that, if they wanted to beat up girls, they were going to get hurt too. They all backed off. The guy on the ground just kept screaming at them, calling them faggots. We just kept standing there ready, cursing like hell. Finally, one of them turned to the guy on the ground and started laughing at him. Soon, they all thought it was funny that a kid, and a girl no less, had knocked his teeth out with one blow. We started laughing, too, and calling him chicken, because we knew he wouldn't do anything without his friends backing him up. When we finally split, we made sure to keep our belts in our hands just in case his buddies changed their minds.

Things didn't always turn out so well. Years later when I was pretty much grown up and I had learned to be scared just like everybody else, my sister and I were walking a friend of ours to the subway station. Fox Street had already gotten the nickname of Korea, and it wasn't safe for a woman to walk alone in the streets, especially not a Paddy. Well, we walked past the subway station nearest us because we were having a good time talking. We kept walking and talking until we found ourselves at the Elder Avenue station, which was elevated. It was getting dark, and we decided that we shouldn't walk any further. As we went up the stairs, we noticed three men walking behind us. Well, they started calling out obscenities to us. At first, we ignored them. As we stood on the platform waiting for the train, the three men came up to us. They continued to be vulgar, but we weren't about to challenge them. But then, one of them grabbed my sister's ass, and all hell broke loose.

I remember how scared I was as we fought those men, mainly because I was so afraid that one of us would fall onto the tracks. We fought them as we screamed for help to the other people on the platform who just watched us getting our asses whipped. I remember there was this one big guy who was impossible to fight. The other two guys were smaller, and with them we might have had a chance. But that big guy just swatted us like flies. One of them picked up a bottle and threw it at us. I put my hands up in front of my sister's face just in time to stop her from getting her face all cut up. My hands were completely filled with blood, and I kept yelling to my sister and friend to run. I knew that the only way not to get killed was to get the hell out of that station. We started for the stairs, when one of the men punched our friend in the nose, and she hit the ground. We ran back, and my sister kicked that man in the balls. My friend got up, and we all ran towards the stairs, fighting them off. The last contact we had with them was as I ran down the stairs, the big guy grabbed me by the back of my blouse, and I found myself running in the air. My blouse ripped off my back, and I was able to get free.

We ran to the token seller and yelled at him to call the police. He just looked at us as if we were crazy. We didn't dare wait around to argue with him because we were sure those three machos were coming down after us. We ended up running down the stairs out of the station and onto the street. We ran a few blocks until we felt safe and then took inventory of our bruises. We walked over to the little square at Hunts Point and washed the blood off with water from the drinking fountain. We knew we couldn't go home bleeding, because my mother would have had an attack seeing us all messed up like that. All I kept thinking as we walked home was how lucky we were that none of us fell or were pushed onto the tracks.

What these men got out of flipping women, I have no idea. Maybe they just had to keep proving to themselves that they were men. I remember walking into my building once toward our apartment, and someone came up behind me and flipped me. I turned to swing, and what stood in front of me was a kid who couldn't have been more than seven years old. My first instinct was to bust out laughing at the sight of this little kid who was already imitating a man. Instead, I grabbed him around the neck and scared the shit out of him. Maybe I had no right to scare him so badly, but somebody had to show him it was wrong before he grew up to be a macho man, too.

I was twelve years old when I started junior high, but I had already mastered the techniques of the garrison belt along with the art of using a comb as effectively as a knife. You always carried a comb in your back pocket in case of emergencies. The technique of whipping it out and holding it at the right angle, aiming straight for the face, was important if anyone would come at you with a knife. There was also the art of making brass knuckles from garbage can handles and, most important of all, the making of your very own zip gun, those junk weapons I mentioned earlier. All it took to make one was a couple of dollars for a toy gun, an antenna ripped off a car and filed down, a few rubber bands and some tape. After that, all you'd need was a little bit of privacy, either a rooftop or a basement, to put the whole thing together. Bullets were easy to come by. There was no law about buying .22 bullets from any hobby shop. There were only laws against buying guns.

The first time I brought a zip gun into the house, I was scared that my mother would find it. If she did, she'd find a way to use it on me. So, I packed it up in a shoebox along with some socks and hid it in the bottom of my closet, just in case I'd ever need it for a rumble. Using a zip gun during a rumble meant that sometimes the gun wouldn't work, but every so often it did, and someone would get shot, even killed.

I was part of a gang, a ridiculous group called the "Satans," who were nothing more than a minor version of the "Royals," made up of our older brothers and sisters mostly. They went on to become the "Royal Sinners" and eventually the "Young Sinners." But we thought we were cool with our red jerseys and the word "Satans" printed in black. We walked around tough, picking on kids who looked like they couldn't fight and having minor rumbles with other minor gangs.

We learned how to walk hunched over slightly, as we sort of bopped down the street. Your walk was very important at that time. The badder you walked, the tougher you looked. The word "man" became part of almost every sentence that came out of our mouths. "Man" and "diggit" and all kinds of ridiculous words. You learned when somebody said something was "bad," it meant that it was "good." You leaned to do a "mean" this or that, which meant that you did it fantastically. And you learned how to slur those words almost like a junkie talked. Thank God, as I got older, I learned to drop all of those words from my vocabulary, not like some of my friends who went on to be parents and who would talk to their kids in all of their bop talk as if they were still walking bad down the street.

The "Satans" were a young group, and since girls mature faster than boys, most of the "Satan debs" started going steady with the "Royals" and soon became the "Royal Debs." We started going out with the older guys, and that meant falling in love for some of us. It also meant carrying your boyfriend's piece (gun) on the way to a rumble, because the cops rarely searched the girls. But that was street life and street life was different from school life.

I hated school with a "purple passion," as everyone said back then. To me, it was like going to jail every day. You would sit there for hours learning all sorts of garbage, like geometry and geography, stuff you really didn't care about. I don't know why I hated it as much as I did. Maybe it was because I was intelligent (as my guidance counselor would tell me) or just plain hopeless (as my teachers would tell me).

There were good teachers and bad ones. The bad ones outnumbered the good by at least five to one. There were a lot of prejudiced teachers in that school, and it came across in many ways, even though some of them tried to hide it. There were some nice little white American girls in our classes, and they immediately became the teachers' pets. They all got to go to the blackboard and read their reports to the class to show how smart they were. They became the monitors. They were never questioned when they raised their hands to leave the room. I never knew why it was so impossible to believe that a Latino kid had to go take a leak just as bad as an American kid. Don't get me wrong when I say American. I was born here and very proud to be American, too, but somehow being a Latino meant you were never really American to some people.

Well, my bladder has always been weak, even when I was a little kid. After raising my hand and calling out to the teacher, saying that I really had to go, and she would just ignore my presence, and I'd finally just walk out of the room. Then, of course, I was marked down in that damned demerit book that each teacher had. Sometimes, yes, I did deserve demerits. I was no angel, but some teachers were fanatic about those demerits. I remember telling my guidance counselor that I didn't deserve the twenty-five demerits I'd get each week. It took a long time to convince her, but I finally was able to prove that one teacher in particular used to give me five demerits a day, whether I was there or not. It had become a habit with her. After checking my absence record with the demerit book my guidance counselor finally let me in on the fact that there was something very wrong with the teacher's mind. The counselor said, however, that I should make the best of it and ignore the teacher, and the counselor, for their part, would ignore any demerits I got from that teacher.

It was very hard to ignore that teacher, however, because she wanted me out of her class, out of the school and quite possibly out of the country. She even threatened to quit if they didn't throw me out of school. I remember that it bugged her that I would get high marks on her tests and as a result she couldn't get rid of me. The whole conflict built up into our own little war. She'd give a test and throw out some nasty remark while standing over me. I'd slap my pencil down, thinking "fuck the test," and she'd make a huge zero on my paper covering the whole sheet. Finally, when she had collected enough of those zeroes, it was time for her to try to get rid of me.

The one thing that she didn't count on was that I had spoken to my mother many times about her. I had told Mom about how rude she was and how she used to pick on me. My mother, knowing that I could be bad when I wanted to, believed me only halfway. She decided to go to school and meet with the teacher herself. She wasn't going to just take my word for it. When Mom went to the school and the teacher was called out of the classroom to meet with her, I stayed in the classroom. I found out what happened because one of my friends was a monitor in the principal's office and she told me what went on.

The teacher walked into the office smiling and said, "How do you do?" Everything was fine until the principal introduced my mother to the teacher. Until that moment, the teacher was very gracious, but as soon as she found out whose mother she was speaking to, she said she didn't have time to speak to her and that if she wanted to meet, my mother would have to make an appointment. Then, she just walked away. The one thing that no one in their right mind should ever do to my mother is treat her like shit. What followed was an all-out argument, with my mother coming out on top, of course. Had that teacher just treated my mother with an ounce of respect, she might have gotten away with her attempt to have me thrown out. Instead, my mother threatened to stop the whole graduation, if necessary, and to call out all kinds of little things that were going on in that school to the attention of the board of education. Among the things she enumerated were the various alcoholics nipping between classes. We all knew about them because the monitors who cleaned out some of the big deals' desks would tell us and we often saw them wobbling back and forth in the halls and heard them slurring their lessons. According to my friend, everyone involved gasped, knowing what she was talking about. The administrators politely told the teacher that if she felt she must quit, as she had threatened, then she should. Only she didn't.

There were good teachers as well, such as my history teacher. She was tough as nails and I liked her, even though I hated history. I never wised off in her class. I remember how she caught me hitting my friend on the head with my books as we walked down the stairs. She hadn't seen my friend hit me first and so she just pulled me out of line and started scolding me while my classmates all went to their next class. I tried to explain what had happened, but she just kept telling me that I could have caused a serious accident and all kinds of terrible things. I felt so bad that I just started crying and couldn't stop. Well, after she saw me crying, she felt bad that she had made such a big stink about the whole incident and she lent me her handkerchief. I felt even worse because she was being so nice that I started crying even harder.

Anyway, as my history teacher kept talking to me, trying to calm me down, my other teacher, the one whose class

I was supposed to be attending, came out of her room to see what was keeping me. My history teacher took her aside and told her that I'd be right in and that I was very upset at the time. "Hah!" said my other teacher, "She couldn't be upset if an atom bomb went off under her chair." I had never seen my history teacher as mad as she was when she lit into that other teacher like there was no tomorrow. It was rare when a teacher would defend a pupil against another teacher, but she did, and I loved her for it.

One of my favorite teachers was my homeroom teacher, who also taught stagecraft to anybody who wanted to learn it. She was a young woman who wore her hair in a ponytail, just like most of us. Everybody liked her, except for a couple of the teachers who were jealous of her popularity with the students. One day in her classroom—I was the closet monitor—the girls from the class next door came to put their coats in our closet. There was a shortage of closets, so we shared ours with the other class. The teacher wasn't around yet, so I was fooling around chasing one of my friends with a blackboard eraser, when I ran smack into this big American girl from the other class. It was an accident and I apologized and went about my business. She went back into her own room. A few minutes later the girl stood at the door of my classroom calling for me to come into the hall. All my friends were watching me to see if I was chicken or not. Of course, I walked boldly out of the room and met not one big girl but two. She had a twin sister who was just as big as she was. I thought I would get killed, but I couldn't back out. They challenged me, and I fought them. I was bounced around a lot, and I bounced them around, too. At one point, when one of them had me by the neck and the other was holding me by the waist, the teacher walked in and separated us all. Then she marched the three of us down to the vice-principal's office. I thought she was so unfair because I hadn't started it and argued with her all the way.

The twins had been in a lot of trouble before and the vice principal threatened them with suspension. Since it was my first time, at that time, he let me go with just a warning. When I was back in my classroom, I sat there giving my favorite teacher dirty looks, pouting and feeling hurt. After class, she called me over and told me to try to understand that it was her duty to report me. I simply listened to her, not understanding what the hell this duty was. Then to top it off, she smiled and said, "Besides, I had to break up the fight because those two girls would have killed you." I thought about arguing with her about that point, until I remembered the position I was in when she stopped the fight. I cracked up laughing, knowing she was right, and we became friends again.

In the ninth grade, I made up my mind that I wanted to be a psychiatrist. I used to go to the Hunts Point Library after school or when I was playing hooky. There I read all the books I could on psychiatry. It wasn't too hard to read them all because there weren't that many. Anyway, I read every one of them, understanding only what I could at that time, and decided that I would make a terrific psychiatrist.

I was able to convince my father to give me the old file cabinet he had in his yard and, from that moment on, I kept files on all my friends and teachers. It was fun talking to them and then writing up notes at the end of the day on this one's schizophrenia or that one's masochism. I thought I was fantastic at it, and a lot of the kids would ask me what was wrong with them, but I of course wouldn't tell them. That wasn't proper. At least that's not how it was done in the movies. You were supposed to say, "What do you think is wrong with you?" Or when they would ask if I thought they were sick, I would say, "Do you think you're sick?" My teachers weren't crazy about my keeping a file on them, but there wasn't too much they could do about it. The file was in my home and was none of their business.

I noticed one thing, though. After they found out about my files, they all became a little nicer when they argued with me. Sometimes when a teacher would yell at me, I'd start scribbling on a sheet of paper, and that would just about flip them out. Sometimes I did take notes; sometimes I just pretended to write as I observed them clinically. You see, as I said before, I was no angel. In fact, sometimes I was a downright bitch.

IX

I was four years old the first time my father ever hit me. It is the first recollection I have of my childhood. I used to like to read, or at least look at the pictures in books, thinking I was reading. Well, that one day, it was bedtime and my father told me to go to bed. Since I was "reading" in the living room, I refused to go to bed until I had finished. He kept telling me to go to bed, and I kept telling him I wasn't through reading. Then he said that unless I went to bed, he would spank me. I told him that if he hit me, I would throw the book at him. He thought it was funny that this little shrimp of his would challenge him. He warned me that if I threw the book, he'd give it to me good. Well, I stood up and warned him, and *he* warned me. After a few warnings, I hauled off and threw the book at him. In turn, he whacked my butt until I cried and ran off to bed.

About ten minutes later, he walked into the room, feeling all guilty. He apologized to me. I told him he should be sorry and, *BANG,* my father hit me for the second time. I guess that's my first childhood recollection not only because it was the first time Pop hit me, but because it turned into a doubleheader.

I always enjoyed reading, and it got me into trouble more than once in my life. When I found about a great store on Hunts Point that kept pocketbooks in racks out front, I'd pass by after school every day and browse the new selections until I found one that looked interesting to me. Then I'd shove it in my jacket and split. This went on for a couple of months and could have gone on forever, if a friend of mine hadn't insisted on knowing where I got all the good books from. Against my better judgment, I told her, and she went with me the next time I decided to enlarge my library. Well, as I was shoving books into my jacket, my pal decided that she could be braver than me. She just grabbed a whole bunch of them in her arms and walked away casually, with the stolen books in plain sight. Of course, she got caught. Because she was my pal, I hung around the store while the man called the police. I had gone into the store to help my friend, and the owner of the place told me to "Get the fuck out." I did but waited to see what was going to happen to my friend.

When a cop finally came and questioned her, she, being the bright girl she was, said I had given her the books. Terrific! The cop called me inside, and I stood there shaking, hoping the books I had in my jacket wouldn't fall out. From that moment on, I became María Santos. That was the name I would use whenever I got caught doing anything bad. Since I had no choice, I told the cop I had given her the books and that I had gotten them from a girl in school. When he asked me why I was standing outside of the store, I politely told him that the owner had told me to "Get the fuck out." He told me to watch my mouth, and I said that I was only repeating what the man had said. After he took down my friend's real name and my fake one, he let us go, warning us that our parents would hear about our being thieves. As we walked out of the store, I swore up and down that I wasn't a thief and that they hadn't caught me doing anything and that I had my rights to be walking around there, and all kinds of other bull.

My friend and I both walked casually down the block. When we hit the corner, we ran like hell, me opening my jacket and letting the books I had stolen fall all over the ground, just in case. I was scared for days after that, worrying that my friend would tell the police my real name if he ever came to her house to tell her parents she was thief. After a while, it was obvious that the cop had no intention of reporting us, and I was able to breathe again.

Reading got me in trouble a few times later in high school. I used to bring a book to class and, whenever I got bored with what I was being taught, I would pick up my book and start reading. This used to make some teachers mad. I had one teacher who was very nice and, even though she wouldn't let me read during her class, she would talk to me about the books I was reading. We'd get into some good discussions. One time, she even borrowed a book of Japanese "Noh" plays from me. That was the first time a teacher ever wanted anything from me other than my scalp, and I was proud as hell. She was one of the rare teachers. She cared about the kids in her class, unlike most teachers I had.

I remember one time in high school I was giving an oral book report to another teacher on the screenplay, "The Misfits." I liked Arthur Miller, but I wasn't crazy about that book in particular. Well, the teacher obviously liked it, and he insisted that I didn't like it because I was a misfit myself. I kept telling him that I wasn't a misfit, and he kept saying things like, "Oh, come on, you know you feel like a misfit." I kept insisting I didn't, and he kept smirking, insisting I was. The class thought it was all very funny, and I started getting angry because this man was making a fool out of me. Well, after a lot of the same question, "You really don't think you're a misfit?" I finally told the teacher to go fuck himself and walked out of his class. Of course, I ended up in the dean's office.

Another teacher sent me to the dean because she saw a book on existentialism on top of my desk along with my regular schoolbooks.

"Do you understand that?" she asked.

"I don't read books I don't understand."

"Oh, I don't believe you," she said.

We went through a whole argument about my brain and her brain, until I ended up explaining existentialism to the dean. Thinking back now, I wonder if I did understand what the hell I was reading. Maybe, maybe not, but at least I tried.

I had a lot of arguments with that same teacher. I remember that she always wore tight dresses, and her front buttons would pop open and everyone could see her bra. Her hair was bleached with peroxide, like the typical dumb blondes you'd see in movies. One time, we had a long argument about England. She said that everyone in England spoke with a cockney accent and I, being the kid who knew everything in the whole world, disagreed with her. After a whole lot of bullshit, I finally let her know that I had lived in England for many years, which was a lot of crap—I had never left New York—and that the cockney accent was spoken by the lower class.

"And because you've also been to England, Miss, you must have hung around only with the lower class."

"You go straight down to the dean's office, now, young lady!" she ordered.

The worst battle we ever had was the time she showed us all a film about Venezuela. I had never seen any films on that country, and this one shocked me. The whole film was about tribes of black people living in jungles. After the film, she explained that this was how the Venezuelans lived and what they looked like. Granted, there are tribes in

Venezuela who live in the jungles, but my grandmother was Venezuelan and she never lived in a jungle and she wasn't black.

"Well, I'm like a quarter Venezuelan and I'm not black, either," I challenged her.

"Oh, you can't possibly be Venezuelan! And if your grandmother was from Venezuela, then she couldn't have lived in a house," she countered.

According to her, they all must have lived in the trees and swung from vines.

"Everybody knows, Venezuela has big buildings, like in Caracas, and it's a very rich country. It is loaded with oil," I said.

"No! It's all jungle, and that's final," she insisted.

"Oh, you go to hell."

"Take that filthy mouth and march straight to the dean's office! Now!"

�𝕠𝕗𝕠 �𝕠𝕗𝕠 �𝕠𝕗𝕠

I was a petty thief and used to rob all kinds of small junk from the Five and Ten or the candy store. With my mother around, that was the only kind of thief I could be. I used to envy the other kids who could walk into their houses with almost anything and not be questioned about it. Not me. My mother made sure she knew where everything I brought home came from. It was easy to say that I bought this book with my lunch money, but anything I came home with had better cost no more than the money I had left with in the morning.

One time I thought I would be brave. Most of the kids around the block had bicycles that they had robbed, and I wanted a bike, too. I devised a plan to get around my mother after I robbed a beautiful green racer that was lying against a building a few blocks away. I walked into the house and told my mother that a kid had sold it to me for two bucks. When she asked me how I got the two dollars, I said I hadn't paid him yet and asked her if she would lend me the money. She was very nice about the whole thing and told me to bring the kid to the house so that she could be sure that he really wanted to sell it. I thought I had it made but I should have realized that my mother was no dummy. I went downstairs and got a group of my friends to back up my story, and one kid agreed to say that he sold it to me.

Well, there we were, the whole group of us, lying like hell to Mom as she listened to why the kid wanted to sell the bike and all kinds of bull. Then she asked the kid where he lived so that she could give the money to his mother. We all died right there, knowing we were caught. But we kept on saying that his mother wasn't home and that she had said it would be okay for him to sell it. After a while, my mother told all the kids to leave. Then, very politely, told me to return that bike as fast as I could or she would kill me. I protested, swearing I hadn't stolen it as I found my-self walking the bike out of the house and returning it to the place where I had had found it. When I came back to the house later that evening, she warned me never to try to con her again, with a few shoves here and there for em-phasis. I never brought anything stolen into the house again. At least nothing big.

ෙ෯ ෙ෯ ෙ෯

I got engaged in the Five and Ten to one of the kids I would play hooky with. That day we had both walked through Kresge's stealing all kinds of little junk. First, he put a kerchief on my head. Then, we each took a pair of sun-glasses from one of the counters and put them on and con-tinued walking around the store. We stopped by the counter with the rings that looked like diamonds and he fit the biggest one on my finger and then kissed me on the cheek. I walked out of the store a happily engaged woman, looking

ridiculous with a $1.98 diamond ring on my finger, sun-
glasses over my eyes and a kerchief on my head. We were
both having a wonderful time playing hooky.

A little while later, we got bored. We had nothing else to
do and we decided to be daring by robbing a lady's pocketbook. We must have stood on the corner for over an hour,
waiting for the smallest, tiniest old lady to pass with a
pocketbook. We were both scared because neither of us had
ever done anything like that before and we kept saying,
"You do it. No, *you* do it. No, *you* do it," until we decided that
he would finally do it. After what seemed like forever, an old
lady finally passed us, and we decided that she would be
the one. We both ran up behind her, and he grabbed the
pocketbook. Well, after all our deciding, it turned out that
we picked the wrong one. That old lady held onto her bag
as if she had a million dollars in it, and there was no way
of taking it away from her. She kept screaming, "Cakee,
Cakee," which sounded like she was saying, "Shit" in Spanish, but she wasn't speaking Spanish. I had no idea what
she was saying. Anyway, we just couldn't get that bag away
from her, and we finally started running fast as hell because people were responding to her screaming. We ran and
ran with people chasing us for blocks. Finally, we ducked
into a hallway, scared to death. We decided against trying
it again. It was too dangerous. Had we gotten caught, we
would have been in a mess of trouble. That episode ended
my career as a purse snatcher, thank God. That episode and
the paint-throwing episode are the two things I am most
ashamed of about my youth.

⚜ ⚜ ⚜

I used to love to gamble. I was good at shooting craps
and playing poker. Since nobody ever had money we played
for things, like rings, watches, wallets, shirts, pants,
combs—anything that you had on you. One time when I

was shooting craps in the street with a boy from around the block, I was pretty lucky and won everything but his underwear. He looked ridiculous standing there in his drawers, so after I had cleaned him out, I gave him back his clothes but kept the pocket stuff.

I used to play poker in school with the girls in my class and I'd win a lot of rings and watches, until one of the mothers complained about it. I had to give one of the watches back because the kid kept crying that her mother would kill her. I never kept the jewelry because I never had much use for it. I gave the rings to my older sister, who loved anything that resembled money. The only kind of jewelry I liked was chains around the neck with holy medals on them. I was never crazy about earrings until I grew up, and then I was glad that Mom had sat the three of her daughters down and pierced all of our ears. Most of the mothers around the block did their own ear piercing. Not like now, where everyone goes and has it done commercially and gets a free pair of earrings to go along with the holes in their ears.

Since I didn't like jewelry, it was easy for my sister to con me into handing over any jewelry to her that Mamá had given me. Being the dumb clod that I was as a kid, I would have a hard time explaining to Mom why I let my sister take my rings and jewelry and throw them down the sewer. But then again, Mom always understood because she always said I was a little backwards. The big joke was that when I was a baby, I even used to crawl backwards.

Everybody used to think that was funny and that it was just more proof that I was stupid, but that didn't bother me. In fact, I was always kind of proud. All other babies I had ever seen crawled forwards. I was the only kid in the world that did everything backwards, and that gave me a tremendous amount of distinction.

Whenever I gambled with my brother and sisters, I would cheat. My mother didn't like us to gamble, so we had to pretend that we were playing for nothing, even though we usually played for our allowances. Whenever I would lose all my money, I would bet the nonexistent money in my pocket. If they asked to see it, I would jingle my keys to make them sound like change. They were all as greedy as I was, and they'd let me continue to play. If I lost, I would go into a box my mother had in the closet where she used to keep her money and I'd go back with a ten-dollar bill. My sisters' eyes would bug out and she'd say I robbed it from Mommy. I'd say I didn't, and they'd let me play. Eventually, I would win back my money and theirs and I'd return the ten dollars to my mother's hiding place. It could be called borrowing.

I never really robbed money from my mother. It was different with my father, though. He was always accusing everyone in the house of robbing him, even when we didn't. So, I decided, "Why not?" He was real tricky, though, so you had to catch him right after he finished taking a shower. As soon as he'd come out of the bathroom, I'd run inside and go through the pants that he would leave on the bathroom floor. This had to be done quickly, because a few minutes later, he would go back into the bathroom and clean out his pockets of all the bills and hide his money, mostly behind the tub or in the hamper and sometimes under his pillow or some other crappy place.

Once he would hide it, you knew that he had counted it, so you didn't touch it.

One morning we all woke up to him screaming that he had been robbed of all his money. We swore up and down that we hadn't done it. He was furious and it led to a big fight in the house. After he went to work, we all searched the house, including my mother, looking for his money. We never found it, and everyone kept swearing they didn't take it. Well, when my mother went to make us breakfast and she pulled out the box of eggs from the refrigerator, there inside the box was his money. The four of us kids voted unanimously that we should keep it because we had been accused of stealing it anyway. Mom voted against it, and her one vote carried more weight than our four. Pop got his money back, along with a lecture from Mom and a lot of dirty looks from us.

I continued to rob his pockets for a while and was becoming a big spender. I would treat my friends to all kinds of good things. Everything was terrific for a while, until one day after playing hooky with a few girls and spending the day in one of the girl's houses, somebody lost their watch. No one was sure who had taken it, and everyone suspected everyone else. A couple of days later, one of my pals came to talk to me about something on the roof. I went along, not expecting to find a reception committee up there waiting for me. They had all deduced that, since I always had so much spending money, that I had to be the watch thief. It was all very friendly at first with just a few friends saying, "Return the watch and nothing will happen to you." I kept telling them I didn't have it.

Then came the threat of, "How would I like to fly off the roof"?

"If I fly, a few of you will fly with me."

I was more angry than scared. I mean, these were supposed to be my friends, and here they were accusing me of robbing one of them. You had to be pretty low to rob one of your friends. (It was different with your parents. Everybody stole from their parents now and then.) Most of them didn't want to believe that I was the thief, but how else could they explain my sudden wealth? Finally, I confided in them that the money I got was from my father's pants, and they all believed me. I was embarrassed to have to tell them that I had taken the money from my father. After that, I didn't rob Pop anymore. I settled for my weekly allowance instead.

All of us kids had itchy fingers in our house. One time when my brother was small, my mother lost ten dollars. She said she had it in her pocketbook, and so we were all questioned. My little brother, in the meantime, took the ten-dollar bill to the candy store around the corner and bought ten dolls and gave all his little girlfriends a doll each. Nobody could explain the missing ten dollars until we found some of his girlfriends playing with the dolls that he had given them. Mom found out about the dolls, collected all ten of them and marched around to the candy store where she retrieved her ten dollars. To this day, my brother insists that he was just sitting under the kitchen table and the ten dollars just flew into his hands. Money from heaven.

Some of the kids around the block were real thieves. A lot of the girls would go to the big department stores with shopping bags and collect a whole new wardrobe. The kids who were turning into junkies were starting to rob apartments. One time I was in my friend's house, when her brother walked in with a big box of baby clothes. My friend's mother didn't ask him where he got the clothes. She just went through them all, saying how pretty this was and how cute that was. A few minutes later, a cop came to the house and arrested him. It seems that he had stolen the clothes from the back seat of a car. All the baby clothes went back into the box, and the cop took the box along with the boy off to the station house.

Stealing was not the only way we made money. We did a lot of selling to make money too. We'd sell Kool-Aid, comic books and just about anything we could get our hands on. My brother was very good at selling things. He could sell anything, no matter how beat up it was.

One time, I threw out a whole bunch of 78-RPM records that were all scratched and worn out. He grabbed them out of the garbage and said I was crazy for throwing them out. He sold them for ten cents apiece to the super of the building, who thought they were terrific.

The most fun I ever had selling anything was when my grandfather brought around boxes full of carnations and we sold them on the corner of Prospect Avenue on Mother's Day. We sold red ones for living mothers and white ones for dead mothers. My mother had a fit with grandpa because she didn't like us selling anything in the streets, not even flowers. We took in a lot of money that day. When it got dark, my grandfather took my sister and me into a few of the bars around the area, saying we were orphans and how selling flowers was our only means of support. He had everybody weeping for us. We were pretty good too, looking real sad into the box of flowers, trying not to bust out laughing. We never told Mom about going into the bars, because she would have killed us. Grandpa, too.

I remember one of the many times that we were going to move away from Fox Street and Grandpa convinced my mother that she could sell her apartment for a lot of money. He was such a great salesman, how he walked people around the apartment pointing out all the good things they would be getting if they offered a good price.

"Look at this beautiful washing machine," he would say. "Where are you going to move to that has a beautiful washing machine like this?"

Of course, the washing machine had been broken for over a year. Then he'd point out the beautiful television and go through the same thing, while we giggled in the background knowing that the TV was also broken. He made our apartment sound fantastic, and someone actually offered $1,000 dollars for it. We rolled on the floor in the bathroom, laughing our heads off. None of us would have given a nickel for that dump, and here he was being offered all this money. Anyway, we didn't move, so nobody got anything.

The only grandfather we ever knew wasn't really our grandfather, though. He was my mother's stepfather. Her real father had died, and Grandma married again when she came to New York. Anyway, the grandfather that we knew looked like a big Jewish man. Very few people could tell he was Puerto Rican. He had a stall at the big market on 116th Street. In those days, most of the stalls were owned by Jewish people. It used to be fun going through the market where you could buy everything cheap. They sold everything there, from food to clothing to fish to candles to kitchen utensils to saints to just about everything. Grandpa used to sell clothing and junk in his stall. He often got into fights with Latinos who would think he was Jewish. They would start saying things in Spanish like, "This Jew is trying to cheat us," and he'd let them go on and on hanging themselves before he would cut loose with the dirtiest Latino curse words imaginable. They'd run off embarrassed as hell.

My grandmother was very different. She very rarely said a curse word, and when she did, it came as a big shock to everyone. One time, I was on the subway with her and, as she went to sit down, she bumped into this woman who was already seated. She apologized, and the woman just turned away from her as if she had just been approached with a bag of shit. Well, my grandmother just sat there with a furious look on her face. I kept asking her what was wrong, but she wouldn't say anything. When it came time to get off the train, I went to hold the door open and my grandmother stood up and looked at the nasty woman. In perfect broken English she said, "Ju can go fuckee juself eef ju think ju sheet don smell like everybody else," and she walked proudly off the train. That was the first time I ever heard Grandma curse, and I thought I would die laughing.

Grandma was a very proud woman who in turn ended up with very proud children, who in turn ended up with proud children of their own. Maybe that's why none of us went on to become whores or junkies like a lot of our friends did.

X

People started locking their doors as more people became junkies and more people were being robbed. Our apartment never got robbed. Maybe it was because we knew most of the junkies around the block and there was some kind of a hands-off policy on our place. One junkie who none of us knew too well grabbed my older sister by the throat one day in our hallway and threatened to kill her. She ran upstairs hysterical and told Mom, and Mom went into a fit. The guy that grabbed my sister lived in the building right next to ours; in fact, you could see his window from ours. So my sister pointed out the window, and my mother started screaming at the top of her lungs for the junkie to show his face. All of the windows in the back opened up, and everyone stuck their heads out to see what was going on. Finally, after a lot of screaming and yelling from Mom, the guy opened his window and stuck his head out. Mom called him every name in the book and threatened to destroy him if he ever walked out on the street again. I guess he believed her, because a short time later he moved out of his apartment, and we never saw him again.

The one thing you couldn't do if you lived on Fox Street was harm one of my mother's children. One time, the super from the next building pulled a knife on my little brother. Mom was down there in a flash and threatened to put the knife up his ass. Then there was the time that a woman hit my sister, and my mother went straight to her apartment and threatened to break her door down and beat the hell out of her. It wasn't that Mom didn't know we were bad or anything like that. She just didn't want anyone else hitting her kids. She always used to tell people, "If my kids do something bad, tell me and I'll hit them, but don't you lay a hand on them yourself."

I didn't mind getting hit half as much as I minded getting punished. Getting punished meant having to stay in the last room all day without watching television or anything. The last room in our railroad apartment was where we kids slept on two sets of bunk beds, that is, until my brother got older, and then he had to sleep in the living room on one of those convertible sofas. Our room was the smallest of the four rooms in the house. It was six by nine feet. The living room and my parent's bedroom were each nine by twelve feet. The kitchen was a little smaller than our bedroom. In the long time that all six of us lived in that apartment we managed somehow not to bump into each other too much or end up hating each other's guts.

One day while I was being punished, I snuck out of the house through the fire escape and rented a bike from the bike shop. When my time was almost up, one of the kids asked me for a ride, and I told him okay, as long as he returned it because my hour was up and I had to get back upstairs. He promised, and I climbed back up the fire escape and in through the window to my bedroom and pretended I had never left. Everything would have worked out fine, if the guy from the bike shop hadn't come knocking on our door a couple of hours later. The kid had never bothered to return the bike. Instead, he and a few of his friends took the bike apart completely and left the different pieces of it all over fire escapes on my block. It was really a drag going outside with my mother and the bike man and having him point out the wheel on one fire escape and the fender on another and the chain on another, until the bike was put together. So, instead of being punished for the day,

I was punished for a couple of weeks. Plus, I had to pay for the damn bike.

That punishment was really rotten, because my mother didn't let any of my friends come to visit me, not even if they came through the fire escape. Some of my friends came anyway, and we'd whisper with each other through the window until my mother would come charging into the room and my friends would scatter up and down the fire escape, some towards the basement, some towards the roof. My mother screaming at them not to come back.

A couple of days into my sentence, she let me out on parole after I promised to be on my best behavior. She didn't like to punish me, because I would mope around the house better than anyone else could. I would drag my head around as if I was all alone in the world. When that didn't work, I would stomp around, as if I were marching in a parade. That trick gave me the nickname "German soldier" in the house.

Things were getting pretty bad around the block. The people in our building were being robbed left and right. One time, my friend was walking into her apartment with her little sister, when she was pulled inside by a guy who was robbing the place. Thank God she was with her sister, because her sister kept pulling her back out with all of her might. They kept screaming and pulling each other, until we heard her from the stoop and went running to her rescue. The guy who was robbing the place gave up his pulling and ran like hell.

Somebody said they found the body of a woman in a garbage can on the way to church, and it became frightening to walk those three blocks at night to go to confession. People started spreading stories about some guy who used to rape kids on the roof, so most of the kids were forbidden to go up on the roof anymore. People were just starting to get scared. We all used to do things in groups. I remember when my sister started going to college at night, we would walk to the subway station and wait for her train, so we could walk her back home.

The kids weren't half as scared as the parents were. We always felt that nothing could happen to us, that is, until it happened. One of the guys was walking home from the bazaar that they used to hold at church every so often when two guys put a knife to his stomach and demanded all of his money. I'll never forget how embarrassed he got. He had been wearing white pants and, when he saw the knife, he got diarrhea. He had to walk home with shit oozing down his bright white pants, past a lot of his friends, who all caught a whiff of him.

A little old Jewish man who lived on the ground floor of our building put up a sign on his door that said, "Please don't rob here because there is nothing to rob." He was robbed a few times anyway. I guess nobody believed him. It was hard to tell who on Fox Street had money and who didn't. Once, there was a big fire in the apartment beneath ours. A lady used to live there, and the only times we ever saw her she would be going through the garbage cans picking up all kinds of rags and junk. When the firemen came to put out the fire in her place, they threw this large trunk out of the window, and thousands of dollars fell out of it. I don't know how many thousands she had, to begin with, but the story went that after the fire she only recovered about half. We assumed the firemen took the rest.

Although the fire was beneath our apartment, they broke down our door and windows. They made a big mess of our house. The fire itself only left a few burn marks around the floorboards. Later on that night, I climbed out of the window onto the fire escape and climbed into the burned-out apartment below, hoping to find some of the missing thousands. The most I found was a couple of burned up Spaldings. I was really disappointed, although I didn't do a very thorough job checking out the place, because it was dark and scary and I was pretty much a chicken.

There were lots of fires around there. We all used to love to watch the firemen put them out. It was really fun when they'd start pouring in water through a hose and the water would come out through the front windows and spray all of us who were standing across the street. One time, a lady was spraying roach spray in her house. Later on, when she was looking for something under her bed with a lighted match, the mattress caught fire. Her whole apartment was toast. Another time, when we were playing ball, we saw smoke inside an apartment on the ground floor. We ran into the building and banged on the door, but nobody answered. Then we ran back outside and tried to pry open the window, but it wouldn't budge. We kept screaming and yelling and were about to break the window, when a lady, who was pregnant, ran into the kitchen from one of the rooms and put out the fire. She must have fallen asleep. Well, afterwards, we all felt proud because we had saved this lady's life. But little by little, we got worried, because we thought we might have scared her into losing the baby. We had seen lots of ladies lose babies from shock in the movies, and we felt guilty that we hadn't been able to open the window and put out the fire ourselves without scaring her. No matter how bright we were, we did a lot of stupid thinking in those days.

Whenever there was a fire on Fox Street there was always a place to stay for the victims of the fire. People would offer their apartments to the victims, even if they didn't know them. There were always a lot of good people around, in case of emergency. People were always giving out food and clothing and furniture, and they helped you to find a new place, no matter who you were. The same thing when some kid would die by getting hit by a car and there was no insurance money to bury him. There were always people to chip in, whether it was a suit to bury the kid in or a few dollars to help pay for the funeral. Every so often, someone would come around with a cigar box, asking for donations to help bury someone in their family.

The one thing my mother always had for us was insurance. That was the one bill she always paid, whether she could afford it or not. We may not have been living in luxury, but she wasn't going to have to beg to let us be buried properly.

Fox Street was changing like mad. I remember how when we were kids, everybody used the dumbwaiter to throw out their garbage. But so many people had been robbed by thieves who would use them to get into apartments that they were all sealed off. Before they were sealed off, I remember how some of us would take trips back and forth in the dumbwaiters with our friends pulling the ropes. That was before we started hearing stories about kids being found dead in them.

Kay's Knitting Store up the corner, where my mother used to knit and purl with the *yentas*, became a hallelujah church. That's what we used to call the storefront churches. We used to look inside through the chipped paint on the window and watch as the people prayed and sometimes had spirits enter them, or at least that's what we thought was happening when they would start shaking or rolling on the floor. Whenever they'd see us peeking in, they'd invite us in to pray with them, but we were too scared to go inside. Besides, if you were Catholic, you weren't supposed to go into other churches. Sometimes, the hallelujahs would stand on the street corners and pray through a microphone and sing all kinds of hymns. We'd have a ball singing with them, even though they all sang in Spanish and we didn't know what the hell we were singing.

The two Jewish grocery stores at the corners became bodegas. Domínguez owned the one up the block and Tommy owned the one down the block. *Cuchifrito* stands blossomed all over the place, and for some strange reason as fast as they'd open, they'd close and then open again. As kids, none of us were crazy about *cuchifritos*. *Cuchifritos* were pig's ears and blood sausage, served with fried plantain bananas and all kinds of stuff that sounded and looked horrible to kids, but ended up tasting delicious as we grew up. Mom loved it all, though.

Some of the candy stores added jukeboxes, and we did a lot of hanging around, listening to rock 'n' roll and smoking cigarettes that we could buy loose for a few cents. They were always Raleigh cigarettes, sold loose because their packs came with coupons and the store owners got to keep the coupons. The first cigarette I ever smoked was an Old Gold. A friend and I lit one up in the backyard and smoked it, having a good old time until we each started accusing each other of not inhaling. Then we choked and coughed our lungs out until we both could prove to each other that we *did* inhale. After that first cigarette we became professionals. The big thing was to do the French inhale, which was to release some smoke from your mouth and then inhale it through your nose. For a long time, whenever anyone saw us smoking, they would see a cloud of smoke coming out of our mouths and running up our noses.

Now that there were no more dumbwaiters, we used to have to throw out our garbage in the basement. Some people were lazy and just threw their garbage out of the windows. We always used to open up our windows and call out the word, "Pig," whenever we saw a bag of garbage sailing by our window and splashing down in the backyard. Some of the supers we had just let the garbage pile up back there but we had this one super named Carlos who used to check the bags to find a clue to who had tossed the garbage. Then, he'd take the bag back up to the people's apartment and give them hell, threatening them with eviction as he threw the garbage back into their house. The whole time that he was the super, very few people threw trash out of the windows, and the backyard stayed clean. When Carlos moved, the garbage began to fly again.

We used to form committees to clean up the streets, and every so often we'd all be out there with brooms sweeping the garbage into the streets. One time, we decided that we should make Fox Street a play street, whether the city or the police or whoever liked it or not. That was after the bartender's kid got hit real bad by a car. He just lay there crushed, screaming and bleeding for what seemed like forever until the ambulance finally showed up. That was the last straw. We set up garbage cans at each end of the street and spread a volleyball net out between them so that no car could enter and run someone down. Some of the drivers made detours and drove down Southern Boulevard instead, but others would just get out of their cars, take down the net and just drive through. Well, we wanted our play street and we weren't going to let these drivers get the best of us, so we set up a committee to take care of the guys who would drive right through. Instead of a volleyball net, we sat right in the middle of the street in a circle at the corner and we sang songs. The drivers would honk their horns, and we'd tell them it was a play street and that they should take the detour. Then, we'd continue to sing. At times this worked, but mostly the drivers would just put their foot on the gas and drive straight at us. We'd have to scatter fast to avoid being run over. After a lot of close calls, we decided a safer plan was necessary. As these drivers would come down the street ignoring our play street signs, a group of us would roll broken bottles and jagged cans out in front of the wheels of the cars and give them some beautiful flat tires. Of course, we had to do a lot of running and hiding, but we were determined to make Fox Street into our play street.

Whenever one of these drivers would park on our block, he got it really bad. We all unscrewed the little caps on the tires and would let out all the air to give him four flats. Then we'd keep the caps from the tires because they made great whistles.

As bad as the block was becoming, we still had fun being kids. We'd walk around harmonizing to the latest songs, until someone would throw a pot of water at us from one of the windows. We also made some great music by banging combs against car fenders and garbage cans. We sounded as good as Tito Puente's band. Well, almost as good. We were always making some kind of good noise. The best noise we always made was on New Year's. Then you could scream and yell and bang anything you wanted to and nobody would complain or throw water on you. Even the cops let you run around the streets screaming all you wanted. I remember that everyone had to be home at midnight, so that they could watch Guy Lombardo on television and wait for that ball to drop in Times Square. You had to be home so you could kiss everyone in your family and scream "Happy New Year" while the grownups would all pray that the New Year would be better than the old one. As soon as all the kissing in our houses was over, everyone would grab a pot and spoons and run through the halls and streets screaming, "Happy New Year!" and kissing everybody they met, whether they knew them or not. It was New Year's, and everybody was always happy on New Year's. There were no enemies, not even kids in rival gangs. We even wished policemen, who were always chasing us or hitting us, a Happy New Year, and they would wish us one back. Everybody was friends as twelve o'clock midnight on January 1st approached, a friendship that even lasted a few screaming hours after everyone went home and the streets were deserted. But later, by the time they woke up the next morning, everyone went back to hating everyone else.

XI

Only a man could have designed the old shape of a box of Kotex. No woman would have made the box that embarrassing to buy, such a distinct shape. No matter what kind of a bag you were carrying, there was no way of hiding that you had a box of Kotex in your hands.

Once you grow up it doesn't matter that much, but when you're a kid and you have to walk past a group of boys on the stoop, you just want to die or make yourself invisible. It was bad enough that when you went to the drugstore, they never used to have sanitary napkins where you could get them yourself, like they do today. They were always behind the counter, and you had to ask the druggist for them. Of course, the druggist was always a man. I remember how I used to whisper, "A box of Kotex, please," so low that the druggist would have to ask, over and over again, what it was that I wanted. Finally, I'd have to say it out loud, and the whole store found out what I was buying. Sometimes you'd hand the druggist a note instead of asking for the Kotex, and he'd look at the note and then at you and smile. That smile that let you know that he knew you had your period. You always tried to give him back a look saying it's not for me, but you never felt it was convincing. Buying it was bad enough, but the big drag was having to walk the gauntlet from the drugstore to your building. All of the boys would whistle and laugh and say, "We know what you got." You had your choice of just ignoring them or saying something like, "Drop dead" or "No, I don't" or "How would you like a punch in the mouth?" No answer helped ease the embarrassment you felt.

Some of the girls around the block began menstruating when they were very young. For others, it took a little longer. I was one of the others, and I remember how jealous I was of the other girls, because most of them had become young ladies, and I was still nothing. Menstruation was something that every girl looked forward to before it would happen to them. It was supposed to be something beautiful, and everyone felt that way until they had it for a few months and realized that they were going to have to go through this crap once a month, every month until they hit change of life, and that was a long way off.

The day I finally became a young lady, I called Mom into the bathroom because I really wasn't sure it was finally happening to me. She assured me that I was now officially a young lady. Then she showed me what to do, while I died of embarrassment. She kept smiling, because I was finally growing up. I don't know why mothers were so proud when that time finally came, but I remember how Mom told her best friend, who was our next-door neighbor, who hugged and congratulated me while I thought I would die of embarrassment. Then, she called up a few of my aunts and, of course, my grandmother.

Grandma promptly told me that I had to be very careful now, because if I even kissed a boy, I would have a baby. Grandma had all kinds of important things to tell me, such as to never by any means let a boy touch my breasts, because that meant he was just pressing the button to open the door. Even though Mom had told us what we had to know, we still had to listen to Grandma's ideas and pretend she was right. With all the warnings and congratulations, the one thing nobody told me was that, to top it off, I was going to have to suffer with cramps once a month, too. Nobody warned me that I was going to break out with acne, either.

Once when I was drinking a Pepsi Cola and my friend was wrestling with one of the P.A.L. teachers, her elbow accidentally hit the bottle I was drinking from and chipped my front tooth. I had trouble enough getting a boyfriend before, but now with my broken tooth, I had an awful time. I had started out being a pretty cute kid, but by the time I hit my teens, I looked like a miniature Mary Astor with a broken front tooth.

I, and every other girl around the block, had a big crush on the leader of the Royal Sinners. He was very handsome, and we were crazy about him. Aside from the fact that he was so good looking, he could also whip anybody on the block. One day, he and a couple of us girls had gone to one of these basement candy stores in another other gang's territory. We were just sitting around doing nothing at the time, when two boys who were both bigger than him walked into the store and challenged him to fight. He very politely excused himself and walked outside with these two Irish guys. I was sure they were going to kill him. Suddenly, he swung his fist into one guy's face and knocked him to the ground and then, *WHACK*, he took care of the other one. The fight lasted only a few seconds.

That was a trick we had all learned as soon as we were able to fight. Be sure to hit the first blow, because that's the most important one. If they hit you first, the odds of you winning really go against you. The thing was to let the other guy talk bad and make all kinds of tough stances, while you kept acting as if you weren't going to fight. That way, he would finally drop his guard as he called you chicken, and then you could land that punch against his jaw that would knock him to the ground. After that, he was shook up and you had the advantage.

Anyway, my crush on the leader of the gang ended as soon as I broke my tooth, and he was cruel enough to give me the nickname "Cara Culo" (Ass Face). That damned nickname stuck with me for quite a while, and the fellas used to get a kick out of teasing me with it all the time. After that, I hated the leader of the Royal Sinners. At least, I hated him until I got my tooth fixed and the nickname disappeared.

My dentist was as bad as any of the other dentists around there. Those guys made a fortune off the poor people in the area, while they did a lousy job on our teeth. I remember how my dentist filed down my front tooth just a little bit too much, so that when he fit the cap over it, it was always loose. That meant that every time I had an argument or spoke out loud, my cap would come flying out of my mouth. It was really a pain, and I had to learn how to curb my temper. Otherwise, my tooth would fall out of my mouth and embarrass the hell out of me. I couldn't even laugh out loud anymore. I learned how to speak out the side of my mouth, and years later when I finally got my tooth fixed properly, it took a long while for me to speak normally again.

Tooth or no tooth I had my share of boyfriends. The kid with the big Adam's apple was my age and so he was too young for me for a while. I went out with the older guys until we were both grown up enough to go steady again. He was the only boy I ever really loved in all the time I lived on Fox Street. When you're a kid, puppy love, as some idiot named it, can hurt very much. I loved him, even though we broke up and he fell in love with another girl, who in turn didn't love him. That's the way love went around there when we were kids. Most of us went out with the ones we didn't love, and because of this, we did a lot of crying.

Whenever there was a set (dance), all the mismatches would really show. They would be there with their boyfriends and girlfriends, hoping that the one they really liked would finally dance with them. Not that there wasn't the good old group who would fall in love with a different girl or guy each week. Many of them were perfectly happy all the time, but there was always that group of kids who would go to the sets and sit around moping. There was one set in particular that I will never forget. My rival wasn't there, so the boy with the Adam's apple that I was crazy about danced every dance with me, just like he had when we were going steady. I remember how happy and sad I felt pretending that everything was the way it used to be. Then, as always, in walked my rival, and that was the end of me. Not that my ex was cold blooded about picking her to dance or that he seemed to forget about me when he did it. It's just that when you're a kid, you don't do things with that grace you acquire as you grow older. You do things solely on emotion.

I didn't want to show him that I felt hurt, so I went outside and sat on the steps in the hallway, feeling sorry for myself. A little while later, he came out and sat down next to me. She had hurt him as badly as he had hurt me, because he loved her as much as I loved him. Since I was always someone you could talk to, he told me how much he loved her. He just broke into tears, and I sat there consoling him, telling him that she really cared for him and that she was just teasing him, even though I knew that she liked someone else. We both sat there on the stairs as he cried, letting out his misery, while I held back my tears. No boy had ever cried so much in front of me before, and I loved him so much more for his vulnerability. When we both finally went back into the set, we danced a few dances together. My rival, seeing things were not going too well for her, decided that she would dance with him. She did, and he was happy. I went home.

I wanted to join the roller derby when I was a kid. I used to love to watch Gerry Murray and Mike Gammon skate. I decided that I would be a roller derby skater too. I bought a pair of great skates, just like the ones the professionals used, and I wore them tied only to the ankle, just like they did. I used to practice like mad at the roller rink that wasn't too far from the Bronx Zoo. But there, they wouldn't let you skate fast. I practiced anyway until they would throw me out for breaking the rules. It used to get me so mad, when I'd have to sit out because a sign would light up for couples only or some other kind of rules. Hell, I paid for the same skating time as the couples did.

Anyway, when I thought I was ready to join the big leagues, I got a release form from the 14th Street Armory, where they used to hold the "Chiefs" matches. I brought it home for my mother to sign. When she saw that the form I gave her said that no one would be held responsible for broken bones or teeth or noses, or any other part of your body, all that ended my roller derby career. I begged her to sign that paper, but she wouldn't hear of it. At the time, I was really upset, but when I think about it now, I have to thank my mother for not letting me ruin my life with another one of my crazy ventures.

I got chased by the cops because they caught me sawing a branch off a tree in a church yard around where we lived. I was up there trying to get a branch to make a bow and arrow, when the cops spotted me. I had to run like hell to get away from them. They chased me with their car until I ducked into an alley. Then, one of them jumped out of the car and chased me on foot through the alley, while the other guy drove the cop car around the block to get me from the other side. That must have been a very important tree, because I never saw the cops move so fast when a crime was committed.

I ducked into the back entrance of a building, ran up to the roof with the cop still behind me and jumped over onto another roof and down the stairs into the street. I hot-footed it home, breaking all kinds of speed records. It was easy outrunning the cops in those days because, aside from the fact that most of them were out of shape, we knew all the entrances and exits to the buildings and all the good hiding places in backyards. Once in a while, though, you got caught. I got caught once by the truant officer. We were all sitting around the street playing hooky, and I didn't know the truant officer for the boy's school. I only knew what the female truant officer looked like. All of a sudden, one of the boys yelled out, "truant officer," and we all split. This other girl and I ran into a building and were making it to the roof, when she fell down and I stumbled over her. She got up, but I couldn't scramble in time.

I had never been caught for playing hooky by a truant officer before. I was sure he was going to take me home and that I'd get killed by my parents. Instead, he took down my name, which was María Santos, of course, and my class number, which was any class but mine, and he let me go. When all of us got back together again, they all laughed at me because I had gotten caught. I yelled at the clumsy girl who had fallen down in front of me, making it easy for the truant officer to catch me. Everybody thought I had "copped a plea," as they said in those days, and I had to argue like mad to prove that I had pulled a fast one on him by giving him the wrong name.

"Copping a plea" meant that you would beg whoever caught you to let you go. It meant that you became chicken and started crying and all kinds of embarrassing stuff. One time we were all running around at a place posted with a "No Trespassing" sign. There was nothing behind the fence except trucks and junk, and we were just having a good time playing follow the leader. Suddenly, some men came out of a little office and started chasing us. They caught my older sister and my friend. We watched from outside the fence to make sure they weren't hurting them as they questioned them as to what they were doing fooling around where it said, "No Trespassing." Well, my sister copped a plea real fast, and they let her go. My friend thought she was cool and wouldn't cry or apologize as long as my sister was there. So, they kept her there, and we all continued to watch. Finally, when they threatened to call the cops on her, she also copped a plea and walked out big and bad, as if she hadn't, but we all cracked up on her. It was really awful having to face your friends, if they thought you were chicken. Sometimes, it was better to just stay tough and take the consequences. Sometimes, your friends could be much worse than the cops.

Someone got dispossessed a few blocks from us. Because none of us knew exactly what "dispossessed" meant, we thought it was great seeing all of this furniture and stuff out in the street, with everyone going through it, looking for all kinds of treasure. One kid found a coffee can filled with coins. He was dumb enough to announce it, and everybody chased him a few blocks until they caught him in a hallway, beat the heck out of him and grabbed the money. My friend and I found a wallet that had some bills in it. We both grabbed it at the same time and agreed to share it. We thought we had hit the jackpot when we saw at least twenty one-dollar bills inside. The only trouble was that the bills didn't look like the dollar bills that we were used to. This one slick girl who was older than us said that her brother would give us fifty cents for each dollar because it was confederate money and was worthless except to collectors. So we, like jerks, sold him all of our dollars for fifty cents apiece, with the exception of a one-dollar bill. We thought it would be cool to have a confederate bill to show off to everybody. Well, as we showed it off, everybody kept telling us that the bill wasn't confederate. It was just old money from years back. We finally got up enough courage to ask a cop if the money was good. He said it was, and then we got furious. No matter, we couldn't find the girl or her brother who had conned us. They disappeared along with our good old money.

People were regularly dispossessed around there, or at least being threatened with a dispossession notices. It was not fair. If you held up your rent, the landlord could have you thrown out without any problem, but if he didn't fix the holes in the ceilings or give you hot water or whatever, there wasn't a damned thing you could do about it. We were handed dispossession notices a few times. Each time, my mother would have to go to see the marshal about it. We used to crack up because the only kind of marshals we knew about were in the movies or on television, and we were very disappointed to find out that the marshal wasn't anything that even resembled a cowboy.

We all acted in a play that was a modern version of "Cinderella." My friend's older sister put the whole thing together. She had some kind of a class in school, where she had to work with kids, and we all volunteered to be in the play. I played one of the ugly stepsisters, and my older sister, of course, played Cinderella, or Cindy as we called her. We had a ball doing it, but more important was that when it was all over, we were rewarded with a trip to see a movie on Broadway. This was a big deal because very few of us had ever seen a Broadway movie, and especially not such a spectacular one as "South Pacific." It was beautiful, with all of the colors changing as Bloody Mary was singing Bali Hai.

There was a big difference between the Broadway movie house and the Ace Theatre. The theatre was decorated to look like we were in Hawaii and the people in the audience were all dressed up to see the show. I remember the only time the movie theatre around our block went out of its way was when it played "Viva Zapata" and all the ushers wore big Mexican sombreros. And there was one other time when a big truck with a colorful tunnel came around the block advertising the "The Tunnel of Love" movie.

The only other time I had seen people dressed up so fabulous was years before, when my mother took us all to the opening of the circus. I remember how people came in limousines and they looked just like movie stars. We kept walking up close to them to see if they were famous. We got so close, we could see the pounds of make-up they had on their faces. We thought they were all pretty ugly, but we loved their clothes and especially their big limousines with chauffeurs. We had only seen chauffeurs in the movies, never real ones. We had more fun watching all of the rich people than we did the circus.

Seeing "South Pacific" had a big effect on me. Maybe it was always inside me, I don't know, but when I saw all of those beautiful colors and heard all of that beautiful music and sat with people whose lives weren't in any way like mine, I realized for the first time that I wanted to be a part of that kind of life. I never wanted to go back to Fox Street again. Fox Street was a prison, and from that day on, all I wanted to do was escape.

XII

The newspapers were having a field day writing articles and headlines about youth gangs. All of a sudden, everything we did became important. The rise in juvenile delinquency and gang wars wasn't nearly as important to us as it seemed to be to the newspapers. The only time it impressed us was when we'd see the name of our gang printed up, as if we were big deals. We used to crack up laughing at them. None of us took them seriously, except to show off.

I'll never forget the time the *Daily News* printed up a big thing about the "Sinners." To impress the newspapers, some of the fellas had painted, "Sinner Territory, Enter at your own Risk," on the side of a building. Of course, the newspaper ate that up and even printed a picture of the warning. It was hysterical to us. Supposedly, we were killers. We were deadly. The newspapers were full of shit.

I won't forget when the "Fordham Baldies" scare went around. This was the first thing that I can remember that was printed in the newspapers about gangs we knew. Supposedly, the "Baldies" were going around to the different schools, attacking girls and beating up or killing kids. We thought that since we had read some of it in the papers, it was true and some of us were scared, at first. All the girls wore dungarees underneath their skirts to school, in case we were going to have to defend ourselves. Our parents were more scared than we were and accompanied their children to school every day. I won't forget the time I was on my way home and I met my mother and my aunt on the way to pick me up. They had heard on the news that the "Baldies" were doing all sorts of weird things. So they came to get me. I was so angry because it made me look like a chicken. And besides, if there was any trouble, I was sure I could handle it better than my mother and my aunt, even though each one of them had a pair of scissors in their pocketbooks.

In school we had a teacher who didn't allow you to wear slacks, so she'd make you lift up your skirt to make sure you didn't have your pants rolled up under it. When we told her that we needed to be dressed properly, just in case, she told us it was nonsense. And as much as we argued with her, she ended up being right.

The "Baldies" scare must have sold a lot of papers, because after that the gangs in our area became famous. Almost overnight, everyone was interested in what gang was fighting what other gang. We all had a ball impressing everyone. Not that gangs weren't dangerous sometimes and that territories didn't mean anything. It's just that the main danger we presented was a danger to ourselves. But according to the newspapers, we were a danger to the community, to New York, and possibly even the nation. Nevertheless, most of us knew that everything we were reading about ourselves was a lot of bull, but it was fun daydreaming. Some of the kids really believed it, though, and went on to stay in gangs even after they had grown up. Most of my friends, however, were out of it by the time we were fifteen or sixteen. It was fun pretending to be the big shots the newspapers were making of us, but deep down we had our heads pretty much together and we knew the difference between fact and fiction.

According to most books and movies I've seen, a "rumble" is supposed to be two gangs squaring off against each other in some deserted place and armed with every kind of weapon imaginable, each gang having planned its own strategy. Then at one point after the gangs have met, all hell is supposed to break loose, like in a war, and the whole thing continues until the cops finally come to break it up. Both gangs are supposed to hate each other and go at it with everything they have.

Hell, reading back what I just wrote sounds just about right, except for the fact that since we all carried zip guns and knives and chains and sticks with razor blades on them, and we did carry all these things into each rumble, how come when the cops would finally come (notice the word *finally*), there weren't at least twenty dead bodies lying all over the street or alley? What seems to be left out of the whole description of a rumble is the human point of it.

True, gangs were groups of kids, but each kid is an individual, and everyone was not out to kill. It was more like "kick ass" time.

I am speaking only for the fights I have seen and have been in, but had we all been the killers that we were made out to be, or the great defenders of our turf, as it was called, and had to fight it out to the end, we all would have been dead or at least crippled. I don't say that once in a while somebody didn't die, but you better believe that if somebody died, it was an accidental death, or one sicko who nobody knew was a killer, had slipped into our midst.

Sure, we all carried zip guns because that was proof of how cool you were, but damnit, it took a lot to use one when you're looking square at another kid, especially since you never intended to be a killer in the first place. You went there to fight and be fought with, but I don't remember anyone I knew who actually went into a rumble with the idea of killing anyone. We weren't killers. We were a bunch of bullshit kids, fighting against each other—I don't care what the newspaper or TV or books said.

Sure, there were kids who killed other kids. I know for a fact that we kept clear of anyone we knew who had actually killed somebody. They were crazy, not us. The only time anyone I knew ever killed anybody, I know it was done in total confusion, and it was a miserable accident.

By the time I was in high school, I stopped hanging around with gangs. The gangs were made up of younger kids, the younger brothers and sisters of our old gang members. I remember how they'd talk cool, just like we had, and how whenever any of these kids had a problem, they'd come to the big guys—sometimes me—to help them out. One day, as I walked out of Morris High School, I could feel that something was going to happen. You can feel these things when you've been involved yourself. I saw some of the younger kids hanging around the school and I asked one of them what was happening. At first, he told me nothing, and then after I called him a bullshit artist, he told me there was a kid who was fooling around with another guy's girl, and they were just going to scare him. After I was given the word that nothing was really going to happen, I went home. A little while later when I was hanging around on the stoop of my building, a few of those kids who had been in front of the school came running up the block, scared. When I asked what had happened, it turned out that instead of scaring the kid, they had killed him. I can still see those kids' faces, crying as they told me what had gone down. They were inconsolable and talked about running away, hiding and doing all sorts of crazy things.

When they calmed down enough, I told them to go to the police before they got caught. It was all an accident, but it would only be worse if they ran away. Well, they finally were picked up, and each of them was arrested and put away as juveniles. Not all of those kids had done the shooting, but they had been there and they were all involved—just as I could have been a few years before.

I knew both the victim and his killer. The victim was a good guy named Johnny. He was in a few of my classes, and he and I used to joke around a lot and get into trouble a little. The kid that killed him was named Eddie and he was a good kid, too. He hadn't hung around too much with the guys before because he went to a Catholic School, but he had finally convinced his mother to let him go to the same school as his friends.

I have no intention of condoning the fact that he killed the other kid because there's no excuse for him pulling the trigger. I do want to tell the truth about what happened, because the newspapers just took the whole story and made whatever the hell they wanted to out of it. The headlines call Eddie "The Burner." It was really sickening to read that about someone you knew who no longer had a name. He was "The Burner" in the headlines and remained so throughout the stories that followed. In those days when you shot someone, it was said you "burned" them, and the newspapers picked up on that nice piece of our language real fast. The shame of it all is not that Eddie turned out to be "The Burner," but that any one of the other kids could have been the burner instead. The same with Johnny, who had been killed. He had lost his life for the worst of reasons, some would say for nothing. None of those guys wanted to do something drastic, like kill him. It was more about scaring him, that's all. No one should have been killed.

The kids that got locked up had been standing outside of the school waiting for Johnny to come out. When he did, they threatened him, and then a fight broke out. They all yelled, "burn him, burn him," and Eddie, who was the one carrying the zip gun at the time, pulled it out and shot one shot in the middle of the chaos. Johnny was dead, just like that. Any of the other kids could have been holding that gun at the time, but it was Eddie who was holding it. It was Eddie who shot it, and it was Eddie who went to prison for it.

Everybody was sick about the whole thing, because both boys were both nice kids. Johnny was dead, and Eddie might as well have died because he went to jail and turned into God knows what by now. What made it really sickening was that it turned out that the guy whose girl Johnny was supposed to be fooling around with was about twenty-three years old, and all of the kids who went to fight for this man's bullshit honor were about fourteen and fifteen years old. That twenty-three-year-old man had conned those kids and got them to do this terrible thing for him. And all he got for participating in the whole event was something like two to five years in jail.

That whole tragedy is so clear in my mind because I remember how I went upstairs into our apartment and I started screaming hysterically. There was nobody there who could control all the anguish that came flying out of me as I tore up my house and cursed Fox Street and cursed my parents for making me live there and cursed the world for making me and my friends go through such misery. I cursed and screamed and hated the damn newspapers and the damn rats and the damn roaches and every damn thing that life had thrown at me and my family and friends. Hell,

I just wanted to tear up everything that was Fox Street or had anything to do with Fox Street. I wanted to burn the whole fucking place down to the ground.

Damn, we were a treat to the newspapers and to the social workers and to the city agencies. We were a social this or a social that. We had tags on us, big tags that said Spics. Spics that shouldn't live like other people or have a chance to grow up like other people. We were Spics who were supposed to be contained in our ghetto with the rest of the garbage. We were Spics doing exactly as we should, killing ourselves off. We were just numbers and statistics to them, but damn it, we were people. We were human beings who loved people as much as anyone else could love people. We cried too. We had emotions too. We liked to laugh as much as the next guy. Instead, we were supposed to be mean as hell without getting out of hand. If you live your lives the way Spics should, then nobody will get upset and try to wipe you out. Live in the filth and enjoy it.

It may sound crazy, but you can enjoy it as long as you remain a kid. You can have a great time until that moment in your life when you finally grow up and then, hell, it's over for you. It's much too hard to find anything funny once you grow up and you're still living on Fox Street. There's not much to laugh about or to enjoy.

I don't mean to say that I grew up when I heard that my friend had killed my other friend.

I was already sixteen or seventeen years old at that time and I had grown up long before then. If you're not grown up by then, living on Fox Street, you're never going to grow up. Oh, you'll still have the same small frame and silly face that you had right before you got hit on the head by the reality of the whole rotten set-up, but inside of that kid body of yours you hurt really bad and hate really strong and love really deeply. There's very little you can do about it, because outside, no matter what kind of brain or instincts you have, you're still a kid, and there's not a damn thing you can do about anything except wait until your body has grown up, too, and you can get the hell out.

XIII

The only way to survive Fox Street was to be away from it for as long as you could, whether it was physically or mentally. Some of the kids around the block were strong enough to do this, sometimes with the help of newfound friends and sometimes all alone. Some kids just couldn't do it and became junkies or ended up in jail or dead. I was one of the fortunate ones.

In school, I was still a little savage to most of my teachers and, at home, I was still just me. On the inside, however, I was becoming a person with dreams and goals and desires that nobody had ever told me I had a right to have. Not that it turned everything into a wonderland. Once you begin to open your mind, it makes you more miserable to see how many beautiful things there are in the world and to realize how few of them are actually yours to enjoy. In fact, it hurts like hell, but that hurting just makes you want to see more, because you realize you have the capacity to feel deeply and to see everything with so much more depth than you ever imagined you could. An example is when I discovered that my favorite painter was Modigliani. Wow, that was a tremendous feeling, looking at a painting and for the first time in my life finding something as artificial as paint and canvas to be one of the most beautiful sights I'd ever seen. If anyone were to ask why, of all artists, Modigliani was my favorite, I couldn't answer. All I knew was that his paintings were able to wipe out the ugliness of the block for me. Edna St. Vincent Millay became my favorite poet. No one had ever captured the beauty of taking that ferry ride for only a nickel, sometimes with someone, sometimes alone, as well as she had in her poem "Recuerdo." I must have recited that poem at least a hundred times. There was always so much sadness in what she wrote, along with so much beauty. She wrote in a way I could understand.

And music for me was a way of escaping Fox Street. Not the rock 'n' roll that was as much a part of the block as the roaches and rats, but classical and jazz. I would go to the Apollo Theatre and for a low-priced ticket was able to see Sarah Vaughn and Gloria Lynne and Ahmad Jamal and other wonderfully talented people. And I used a friend's I.D. to get into the Village Gate to see Nina Simone and John Coltrane. Then, too, I was discovering Beethoven. Reading the jacket covers on the albums and learning little bits of information about the music I was listening to, hearing a beautiful symphony in the background of the film "Goodbye Again," and realizing that it was Brahms' "Third Symphony," running out and buying a copy of Brahms' "Third" conducted by Otto Klemperer, whom I had never heard of before, and discovering more beauty in that music than I had remembered from the film—it was all of this. It was writing a poem to match each movement of the symphony and realizing that the music had made me write a poem.

The first ballet performance I ever saw was actually three different ballet excerpts that the P.A.L. took us to see. One of the dances they did was from "Swan Lake." I remember walking out of City Center, where I had just seen Allegra Kent and Jacques d'Amboise dance for the first time and how a few blocks away there was a film of "Swan Lake" that had been made in Russia. I went straight from seeing "Swan Lake" for the first time to seeing it for the second time, only the second time it was the complete "Swan Lake," danced by Maya Plisetskaya. I memorized her name because she had danced so beautifully, and I had never seen anyone dance like that before. Fox Street disappeared from my mind and stayed out of it until I took the subway home and got off at the Longwood Avenue Station.

There were so many ways of getting away from Fox Street, and I learned every one of them . . . by going down to Greenwich Village and sitting in the park across from New York University . . . or just sitting in a coffee house for hours watching people play chess. At that time the Village was filled with poets and artists (Beatniks as some people called them) and had not yet been taken over by hippies, bums and drug addicts.

You can't imagine how safe and secure a person can feel sitting in a place filled with people who have no idea what it is to live constantly in conflict with others. I mean, there was conflict, but the fighting was intellectual, not physical. After a while, the Village became just another rotten place, because too many people began to use it as their escape, and you ended up meeting the same people you were trying to get away from.

Every escape wasn't as beautiful, and in fact some of my places I ran away to were downright ridiculous, but anything was better than Fox Street. For instance, when I played hooky for three straight months. After going to the Museum of Modern Art one time too many, I decided I needed a change. Because I didn't have much money, I'd go to Times Square and wait until the ushers of the various television shows would hand out free tickets to the daytime quiz shows and variety hours. I saw the Peter Lind Hayes and Mary Healy Show at least forty times. It was not exactly the most exciting show in the world. Anyway, I remember that whenever they'd turn the camera on the audience, I would duck, because I was always sure that my mother would be watching and she'd see me there and kill me when I got home for playing hooky.

When I'd save two days' lunch money, which was two dollars, I could go and see a movie in Times Square. At that time, it was great, because most of the movies opened at nine or ten in the morning and ran continuous showings. I could sit in the movie house all day long. Most of the time, it was great because I never minded seeing the same movie three or four times until three o'clock came around and I had to get home. Once in a while, though, there'd be some creep who'd try to get fresh, and I'd have a big fight, and that would ruin the whole day.

I remember one time, though, that this fat bastard sat next to me. The theatre for the most part was empty, and he just had to sit in the seat right next to me. I, of course, changed my seat because I was used to creeps like him. I won't forget it because this young boy who was a little older than I was turned to me and asked if the fat man had gotten fresh. He was willing to wipe the man out. I told him no, and that I had moved, just in case. Meanwhile, in the back of my mind I was sure the kid was also going to try to get funny. Instead, he started telling me about his life and how he had been in jail for some time and that he had just about given up hope completely until he became involved with a Pentecostal church that had taken him in and how his life had changed because of religion. I wasn't sure whether to buy his story or not, but there was so much honesty in the way he told it that I realized that this was *his* escape, just like I had mine. We talked until the movie was over and then we both said goodbye and never saw each other again.

Playing hooky for three months wasn't exactly the easiest thing to do in a family like mine. I not only had to look out for my mother and father but my father's friends and all our aunts and uncles and my two sisters and brother. The hardest part was to find a way to hide in the hallway waiting for the mailman, because Mom was too slick to give us the mailbox key. I had to hide there, hoping nobody I knew would be coming downstairs at that time. Then I had to get the postcard that the school would send informing my parents that I had been absent.

One day I was fooling around with a whole bunch of kids who were also playing hooky a few blocks away from my home. I had no idea that my family would be out there scouting me. There I was, having a great old time, when I turned and saw my aunt standing at the corner with her hands on her hips. I was caught. My friends scattered because they knew her. She kept screaming to them that she was going to tell all their mothers. Then she took hold of me and marched me to school. I'll never forget how embarrassed I was when she brought me into school and told the people in the office that she had caught me playing hooky.

When I got home, my grandmother, who was taking care of us at the time, just told me to go into the bedroom and wait until my father got home. When he finally came home, he surprised the hell out of me. He didn't hit me. He just sat me down at the kitchen table and told me that he knew that I was playing hooky for at least ten days. I was really glad that he thought it was for that short a time, so I didn't argue with him. Anyway, he did a whole lot of talking about the importance of school, and I did a whole lot of crying, saying how much I hated it and that I never wanted to go back. The talk went on for a long time. I kept saying that I just couldn't go back to school anymore, and he kept saying I had no alternative. It was Thursday already, so I promised to start going back to school on Monday—that was my proposed compromise. He said I would have to go Friday, the next day. I told him that would be impossible, and he promised to beat the hell out of me unless I made it possible. I continued to say no and swore that I would go on Monday. We finally left the whole conversation at a standstill. He wouldn't budge and neither would I.

The next day, Friday, I of course played hooky. It was to be my last day of hooky for a long time, and I made the best of it. After school, when I went home, grandma just pointed to the bedroom and promised me that I would get the beating of my life. She wouldn't tell me why she was so sure of that, no matter how many times I asked her. It didn't take long for me to realize that they had called the school and found out I was absent a lot longer than ten days.

I remember standing on the top of the bunk bed, leaning against the wall as far back as I could, when I heard my father come home. We always used to do this when he was going to hit us, because he wasn't exactly a giant and he couldn't reach us very well. Sometimes after a few swats with a belt he'd finally give up. Not this time, though. He just walked into the room and with one swift leap grabbed me by the corner of my shirt and, *CRASH*, I hit the floor, headfirst. Then he gave it to me with all his might. He had never hit me that hard before, and I was paying for my defiance. At least that's what I thought at first while he kicked me all over the place, but after a while of hearing him yell and scream, I realized that all he was worried about was which boy I had played hooky with. He really didn't care that I had missed school as much as he cared about what guy I had been with and what we had done. I swore to him that I was playing with a group of kids, but he did not believe me. I got the beating of my life.

Getting hit was bad enough, but he topped it off by ripping up my dungaree jacket and my dungarees. They were my prize possessions, and he just tore them to pieces. That was the worst punishment he could have given me, and he forbade me to ever wear pants again. I was grounded for a month and deprived of all kinds of other stuff that I didn't care about.

After about a week of punishment, he relented and said I could go out again. I told him that I couldn't because he had ripped up my only clothes. He was feeling so guilty for the beating he had given me that he gave me money to buy new dungarees and a dungaree jacket. I thanked him and went out and bought my new clothes. Anyone who likes dungarees knows what a drag it is to have to go through the process of making them seem old, because nobody but nobody likes new dungarees. They've got to be worn out and faded before they feel or look comfortable. For a long time, I walked around looking pretty much like a square.

I didn't play hooky much after that beating, until my last year of high school. Then, I finally decided to quit school altogether. My mother did a lot of crying. I just could not stand school anymore, and she knew that if she didn't sign the form for me to drop out, I would just play hooky. I left school and went to work for Kresge's Five and Ten on Southern Boulevard. I made forty dollars a week, less taxes, which made it really about thirty-one dollars a week. After working there for a few months and breaking all kinds of selling records for my counter, "Notions," I finally quit because there was no raise to accompany my great accomplishments. Every week, I passed the sales record and every week I was patted on the back, but no money went along with the pat. I decided I had better go back to school and get my diploma. It really cracks me up to see commercials now on TV telling you not to drop out. You cannot believe the trouble I had trying to get back into school. The people there just refused to accept me, and I had to fight like hell to get back in. Finally, they compromised and made me take my last year with a general course. I graduated with a miserable general diploma. If you've ever tried to get a job or go to college with a general diploma, you'll know the diploma and a token will get you a ride on the subway, not much else.

After high school, I still hung around with my friends and did all the bad things that kids do when they're together. I went to sets and played pool in the P.A.L. and hung around with some of the gang kids. I played stickball in the street and sang songs on the stoop. After a while, though, I realized that I didn't enjoy doing all those things as much as I used to. I was really different from most of the other kids already. I was growing up faster than they were, and we stopped having much in common, except for the fact that we all lived on Fox Street.

Little by little some of the other kids were also growing up, or should I say not accepting the fact that all we had was fighting and playing games and being bad or trying to be cool or whatever. Little by little a new clique was forming and I was becoming part of that group. We were the poets and artists of the block. We weren't an exclusive group, and anybody who wanted to hang around with us could, but not too many kids thought we were as cool as we did. They had more fun living out their lives being tough. Not that we had turned into wishy-washy jerks that anybody could pick on. Hell no. We still could whip anybody that wanted to try to get wise with us, but we no longer provoked the fights and only fought when we were fought with. We still maintained our reputation for being tough. We were just a little weird to everybody.

Instead of hanging around on the stoops doing nothing, we now hung around in each other's homes and wrote poetry and drank tea and painted pictures and wrote songs and listened to music. We took all kinds of new pride in ourselves as we read our poetry aloud and compared ourselves to Rimbaud and Millay and Baudelaire. We read Russian novels and we listened to operas and symphonies. We put our emotions on canvas or in writing and, little by little, Fox Street became our own Left Bank of Paris. And the rats and the roaches all became part of living *la vie bohème.*

XIV

The kid downstairs had a shoot-out with a kid from another gang and, the kid downstairs missed the other guy and shot a lady in the leg by mistake. He ended up in jail.

The kid who used to sing with a very high voice and who used to hang around with us became a junkie.

The girl who lived up the corner and had a whole lot of drug addicts in her family committed suicide.

The family from downstairs moved away after the oldest of the boys was killed in the Army.

A few of the girls I knew became pregnant and either got married at sixteen and seventeen or killed themselves or ended up in reform schools for delinquent girls.

The kid who used to hang around on the stoop all the time and who didn't have too many friends became a wino, then a junkie, and after a while died of an overdose.

A lot of the fellas became thieves to support their habits while a lot of the girls became prostitutes to support theirs. Most of them ended up in jail or dead. Some of them went on programs for drug addicts but as soon as they got back to Fox Street, they went right back into drugs again.

Fox Street was called Korea because people got shot there, as in the Korean War. Longwood Avenue, which was just around the corner, was called Tombstone Territory because the people who got shot on Fox Street somehow managed to run as far as Longwood Avenue before they'd drop dead in the street.

The little park on Hunts Point where my sister, my friend and I had stopped to mend our wounds the time we got jumped on the subway station is now a park exclusively for junkies. They found a guy I knew dead of an overdose on one of the benches there.

The odds of making it out of Fox Street in my time were about fifty-fifty, and I would say that at least fifty percent of the people there made it out okay—nothing spectacular, but at least alive. The other fifty percent went to hell.

The odds of making it out of Fox Street now as I write this, in any kind of a decent form, might as well be zero. I went back to Fox Street about three years ago in order to visit for a few days. There were still kids smiling and lots of singing going on, but all of the misery had multiplied ten times over from when I lived there. Given time, the roaches and mice and rats had multiplied along with the garbage. The buildings are so much more corroded, and the ones that have been burned out by fires are still standing, giving junkies a place to sleep and kids another place to explore.

In the short time that I was there, I saw a man who had been shot dead, lying on the street outside of Nedicks on Westchester Avenue. I don't know if he was the good guy or the bad guy. All I know is that he was dead there with a huge crowd of people standing around his bloodied body.

The man who owned one of the stores on Hunts Point, or maybe he just worked there, was stabbed to death by someone who was trying to rob the store.

There was a big crowd standing in front of where I used to live, and I saw that they were all surrounding a junkie who had overdosed. They were putting ice inside of his clothing, trying to bring him out of it, while at the same time they were trying to get him out of the view of the police, who might come and arrest him.

One day, I looked out of the back window of my apartment and watched as a few fellows climbed out of somebody's basement window carrying records and a stereo and some clothes they had just robbed. If you wanted to buy a gun, all you needed was twenty-five dollars, and a guy with a whole suitcase of them would sell you whatever kind you wanted.

There was a check cashing place about a block away from the Simpson Street Police Station, where the people from the neighborhood would go to cash their welfare checks. Outside, the junkies were lined up just waiting for the people to come out with their money so they could hit them on the head or follow them to their buildings and rob them in the hallways.

Westchester Avenue, right by Hunts Point, was the place where all the prostitutes, who were mostly junkies, would sell themselves for five dollars to any man who could afford it in order to get that much-needed fix.

I had seen so many of these things when I was a kid growing up, but they were spread out during my youth. Now they were happening in rapid succession. There was no time lag between one rotten sight and the next. Things were all happening with a speed that seemed almost impossible in a city that was supposed to be civilized.

There is only sadness when I think of Fox Street now. I think of the good times, but they are mired by the sad ones. As a child, you enjoy everything, but as you grow older, the sad times get in the way. Maybe I did have fun. Then again, maybe I didn't, and it was all an illusion. Whatever it was, it's all I have to remember. It's difficult to get past the sadness. So many people have settled for their lot in life, and mine was just beginning.

BRONX STORIES

FREE FOR ALL

"One from behind the line, five from the middle of the street, ten from across the street and one hundred from the roof."

The young girl strode confidently to the opposite sidewalk, her ponytail bobbing behind her, sweeping the wings of her back. Tiny beads of perspiration glistened on her brown arms as the sun's rays illuminated them.

Lourdes turned to face her challenger, who knew within the depth of his upbringing that no girl could defeat him playing marbles. Up and down the block, neighborhood boys were shooting marbles at opposing player's marbles, winning and losing, oblivious of the threat to their masculine terrain.

Fumbling in the pocket of her two-sizes-too-big dungarees, Lourdes clutched the two stray marbles she had found in the gutter.

"Are you gonna shoot, or aren't you?" the boy yelled at her. "I ain't got all day."

Taking careful aim, Lourdes held the glass ball between her thumb and forefinger, brought her arm back and then quickly thrust it forward.

"Missed!" he jeered as he quickly retrieved the errant marble and shoved it into his pocket.

"Damn!" Lourdes muttered, knowing she had but one more chance to play.

She could not count on finding another one. Too many small boys were out combing the street now, slithering under parked cars to fetch their booty. She couldn't very well ask her mother for money to buy a bag of marbles because playing that in the street was taboo, especially for daddy's little girl. Lourdes was allowed to play house, skip rope, play potsy, but marbles were forbidden "or else."

"Come on, already," the boy shouted, "or give someone else a turn."

Lourdes stared threateningly at the marble in her palm, daring it to miss. She took aim and a deep breath, then released the marble. It found its target.

"Lucky shot," he mumbled as he grudgingly counted out ten marbles and placed them in her hand.

Lourdes had found her mark and knew she wouldn't lose it again. Over and over again, the same transaction took place with other boys. Ten for one, ten for one, ten for one. Her pockets were bursting with marbles, her heart bursting with pride. Her jeans were slipping down from the weight.

"Time out," she called as she adjusted her garrison belt to meet the challenge.

She had caught the eyes of some of the other players who opted to delay their playing in order to watch her. Aloud, they assured themselves that it was pure luck. No girl could play that well, especially no girl that was around the same age as they were. Occasionally she would miss, and they would applaud. But those misses were few and far between. The skill was there. As they came to recognize it, applause came for the hits and groans met the misses.

"Hey man, you're cleaning everybody out," one boy screamed from across the street. "Let someone else go."

"Chickenshit!" Lourdes shouted back, to the amusement of the others.

The younger kids ran back and forth collecting her loot and placing it in a paper bag they had found, because her pockets were now jammed full. She rewarded them with two out of every ten she won.

"I'm out!" came the voice of her current challenger as he counted out his last few marbles. "I only got eight to pay you."

"Keep them," she said sportingly.

"Shove them," he muttered, scattering them in the street to the delight of the younger boys. Spitting at the sidewalk through his teeth as he turned and stormed off.

"Nobody can be that lucky," said another as he placed his marble down, taking up the challenger. "Especially no girl."

The others cheered his bravery and assured themselves of their own by vowing they'd be next, if he lost. The scenes that followed were the same, each new challenger replacing the former. No one left after losing. They just stood there waiting to see their friends defeated and applauding as she picked them off, one by one.

Lourdes noticed, through the corner of her eye, that Armando was watching. He was the only boy on the block who made her tongue-tied when she spoke and feel foolish in his presence. He was not smiling nor cheering her on like the others. He just stood quietly apart.

"You gonna shoot or what?" her new opponent called out.

Lourdes turned to face him. Her concentration had been thrown and she missed the first few shots, only to regain her composure and resume winning.

The sunlight began to wane, and the streets became shadowy. Yet Lourdes persevered. She would show everyone her ability and take on all comers. She was no longer just a girl with a faceless identity. She was part of the group. She had earned her place as the winner.

Lourdes was bursting with joy as she finished off her last opponent. Cheers rang out from her newfound peers, and she gladly accepted the congratulations and the hand-shakes. A couple of boys ran to buy sodas, and the candy store man sent her a complimentary one. He had sold more marbles in one day than he had in months. She was famous and enjoyed every moment of it.

"You didn't win yet," a voice cried out.

Lourdes' stomach knotted up. It was Armando. He stood before her as the ultimate challenge.

Armando placed his marble down on the pavement as she walked across the street, outwardly calm, inwardly trembling.

"You can do it. You can beat him," the boys reassured her, sensing the mental battle taking place.

Armando had never addressed her directly before. She had always been among a group of nonentities to him, one of the girls who happened to be there when he spoke to someone important. Now, he was aware of her, and she flushed with embarrassment.

Her girlfriends who had feigned disinterest up to this time now gathered around to watch her humiliation. They knew, as did he, that she had a crush on him. They had warned her that he didn't like tomboys. He was a rooster and they clucked about him like silly hens.

"I don't want to play anymore," she heard her voice say-ing as she fumbled a marble and watched it drop from her hand.

Cries of "Coward" and "Chicken" rang out from the crowd. Cruel giggles emanated from her friends.

"Play or forfeit," Armando called out, silencing the group about him.

His once boyish grin, which had always been irresistible to Lourdes, now transformed into a sneer.

"You play or you forfeit," he reiterated, staring into her eyes, trying to force his dominance over her.

Lourdes controlled the urge to violently shove the marbles down his throat.

She was humiliated not so much by him but by her own emotions, which had failed her so bitterly. Tears of anger welled in her eyes, and she breathed in deeply in an effort to contain them.

"All or nothing," Lourdes' voice rang out confidently. "Your marbles against all of mine."

All eyes were on him now. Would he take the dare and possibly lose to a girl, or would he walk away and lose the macho rep he had worked so hard to achieve?

"One shot?" Armando asked, his voice faltering.

"That's it. Take it or leave it," she challenged.

Although the sun had gone down and the evening had cooled off, Armando felt the sweat trickle down his forehead and into his eyes. Wiping it away with his forearm, he knelt down and readjusted the marble in the precise position that he wanted it. She watched his unsteady fingers. She could feel the adrenalin of confidence pumping through her veins. Her choice of placement ran unwillingly through her head, but she dispelled all doubt as quickly as she dispelled the marble from her hand.

Crack—the marbles collided with a thunderous sound, scattering wildly. The crowd was in a frenzy as the combatants' eyes met, both mixed with victory and defeat. It had been an inevitable showdown, and someone had to be the victor.

A short while later, the crowd had dissipated, girls and boys going their way. Staring at the open paper bag brimming with marbles, Lourdes listened to the younger boys and girls that surrounded her as they recounted the greatness of her achievements. The girls with newfound confidence boasted that they too could beat the boys if they had a chance. The boys dared them to try. Lourdes saw her hand reach for the overburdened paper bag and quite suddenly thrust its contents into the air.

"Free for all," she shouted as the marbles flew into the air and fell like heavy raindrops against the pavement.

The children scrambled to retrieve as many as possible for themselves.

Sufficiently armed, they set about to defeat each other, each one wanting to be a winner but no one caring who they would have to defeat to win.

Lourdes walked toward her building, holding back her tears, a sad smile pressed across her face.

THE CARD COLLECTOR

Cookie stopped off at the funeral parlor on her way home from school as she did every day. Most of her friends thought it was a ghoulish thing to do, but Cookie didn't care.

"It's just like church," she would say, as their index fingers circled their temples.

Tiptoeing past the office, she knew the funeral director would be taking his usual nap between viewing sessions. He had tossed her out once before, and she did not want a repeat performance of that embarrassing episode when he had accused her of robbing the dead.

"Everyone knows it's the people who work here who really rob the dead," she thought as she entered one of the rooms. She immediately searched through the memorial prayer cards for one to add to her collection. She smiled and pocketed a card of the Infant of Prague.

Cookie turned to look at the figure in the casket. It was a young boy close to her age. Adjusting the rosary in his manicured hands, she said a prayer, then left wondering what color his eyes were.

Several weeks later, July 3rd, 1999, to be exact, after drowning her pancakes with syrup, Cookie glanced up at her father's Sunday paper. There was the same boy staring at her beneath the headline. "Teen Shot by Bodega Owner."

"He's already dead," she screamed. "I saw him a few weeks ago. He was laid out and everything."

"You and your imagination. You're a little loopy if you ask me," her father said, tousling her hair and putting her in a headlock.

"No. I swear. Wait, I'll prove it to you."

Rummaging through her prayer card collection, she found the Infant of Prague and was shocked to find that the date of death read July 2nd, 1999.

THE SÉANCE

Joseph sat squirming in the aluminum chair he had been assigned, wondering how he had allowed his wife, Julie, to convince him to come to a séance in "bongo land," which was his warped term of endearment for the South Bronx. "They'll probably steal my car, and we'll have to get a police escort out of there."

He had done everything, short of commitment to an institution, to ease Julie's pain from the loss of their only child. He had gone to meetings and shared stories with others in similar situations. He had spoken with therapists. He had returned to the church and made weekly visits to the cemetery, and not once did he gripe about their non-existent sex life.

Once at the séance, the old woman who led the gathering spoke her "Latino gibberish," at the same time splashing him and the others with holy water.

He could not help but feel that this was the last straw. "Life has to go on," he thought, "and this is not the way I plan on living it."

Joseph was glad, as the lights were lowered, that he had been seated next to a beautiful blonde stranger, who appeared quite out of place at the table. Eager to hold her lovely hand as the ritual began, he felt his flesh crawl as he listened to his wife speaking to the old hag as if she were talking to their dead child. He was equally appalled when a little voice responded to her from this charlatan's mouth. It was only the touch of this beautiful stranger that kept him from releasing his rage at the ridiculous spectacle.

"It must be my imagination," he mused as the woman beside him appeared to flirt with him in the candle-lit shadows.

Trying to discern her features, he could see that she had lovely oval eyes and lips that would entice any man, let alone one who had not felt the gentle caress of a woman in years. Lips that he knew would be sweet as nectar to the taste played with his imagination. Joseph allowed himself to daydream of a world he and this ravishing woman would share.

Disturbed by the cruel light that brought him back to grim reality, Joseph looked down at the hand that had mesmerized him, only to find his hand intertwined with the wrinkled flesh of the old woman conducting the séance.

With a knowing smile, she spoke her final and only word to him: "*Adiós.*"

THE RED BANDANA

Lucy listened with deaf ears to Msgr. McDermott's eulogy, silently questioning why his God had not protected her son. Her throat was sore from holding back tears she would not shed among strangers, who would expect a spectacle of emotions she would not provide.

As the others fingered rosary beads, she was content to reach into her pocket, every now and then, to touch the last *Star Wars* figure she had purchased for his collection. She remembered that he would have yelled at her for removing it from its hard plastic wrapper, diminishing its worth as a collectible.

"So many friends," she thought, as the procession of endless mourners filed by the casket. Occasionally a familiar face would come into her blurred vision, but many others were strangers. She had always made it a point to know the people her son had hung out with, but time spent with her son had become a rare commodity when it became clear that her job and the much-needed wages she earned were so important to their survival.

It was only after the Monsignor, who had baptized her only child just fifteen years earlier, had given his condolences and left that she addressed her son one final time. Straightening the out of place strand of hair that he had always groomed carefully, she noticed the hint of red placed in his pocket by one of those that had wept before her very eyes. Carefully she took it into her hand and felt the rage burst from her body. The red bandanna fell from her hands as she realized that her child had been baptized by the streets.

JUNIOR HIGH GEMINI

The two-headed monster, the Tweedledee and Twee-dledum of nonfiction existence, entered my life, smoke pouring from its noses, belching city bus exhaust fumes. Surely it would pretzel my small form and ship me home draped in the American flag. She was Goliath opposing an unarmed David. My slingshot. Scratch that! My kingdom for a hand grenade.

Instinct summons. On your knees, fool, and pray for forgiveness from the Lord.

"Forgive me, Father, though I don't know what I've done."

Perhaps the sin of pride, you foolish blowhard, so proud to monitor the homeroom closet, protecting juvenile jackets and galoshes from unscrupulous predators. My first important position in life showed signs of being my last.

Granted, I had been derelict in my duties, by chasing after one of my peers, which led us both out of the classroom. But that could only be classified as a youthful foible, certainly not a mortal sin. "Thou shall not skylark," had not been carved in granite. Besides, the chase had been precipitated by a well-aimed blow to my head by a chalk-filled blackboard eraser.

Had I known what awaited me in the outer limits, I would have undoubtedly remained within, retaliating perhaps, by revealing a very ugly tongue to my friendly adversary, for valor was a gift never bestowed upon me.

Running freely into what should have been open space, I collided, head- on, with a brick wall, or what I assumed was a brick wall. As my bones settled back into place and my vision slowly cleared, my brick wall began its metamorphosis into human form.

In less than a second, I was able to discern that the gargantuan figure that loomed over me was an older pupil, larger than a teacher, who no doubt favored the death penalty for any crime. With my animal instinct for survival, I blurted out an apology, concurrently whispering three Hail Mary's. I waited for acceptance, like a dog does for a bone, and was moved to tears of joy when this leviathan made an about-face and disappeared quickly down the hall.

Lest she change her mind, I collected myself, post-haste, and flew back into the room, depositing my trembling body into the first unoccupied seat I could find. I have learned through experience that spending hours worrying about impending doom, ensures the fact that nothing will happen. However, the same premise must be applied to the opposite. Not worrying has a way of sneaking up on you and shocking you out of your bloomers. Being inexperienced, I chose to forget the unfortunate incident and eased into a dialogue with my peers about the latest on *American Bandstand*.

Silence is a warning, and my entire class became instantaneously mute, all eyes on the doorway. Assuming they were enthralled by my infinite knowledge, I prattled on, until I felt a deadly chill run down my yellow spine. Doomsday had arrived.

Six feet, the least, I jumped when I faced my enemy and saw that she was verily cut in half, for glaring at me were her two beady eyes, but from opposite sides of the doorway. It was at that precise moment that my brain ordered me to vomit, but my body thankfully disobeyed. A Herculean digit, followed by an even more Herculean hand, signaled me to rise and meet it. Compelled to obey, I entered the arena like a true Christian about to face the lions. If one should be thankful for small favors, I was somewhat relieved to find that my two mythological Cyclopes were a twin set of mortals, with four eyes between them.

I felt obliged to answer in the negative all questions shouted at the top of my head.

No, I wasn't looking for a fight. No, I didn't think I was so tough. No, I wasn't smart at all.

No, I didn't want my teeth knocked out.

My negativity could have continued to this day, for I was in no hurry to meet the Grim Reaper. However, my classmates felt differently about my destiny. All of them agreed I should trounce the bullies. More painful than physical injury is the pain of being awarded the cognomen of "poltroon" by one's peers. So throwing caution to the wind, and sanity out of the window, I closed my eyes and came out swinging.

I forgot that this duo was ten feet taller than me. In a flash I became the Manassas Mauler.

I weaved, then I jabbed, first a left, then a right.

I blackened an eye. What a glorious fight.

When the teacher entered, God love her, my adversaries were in the process of evening up the odds, for one held my arms and the other my legs. Each one pulled, trying to stretch me to their size.

I thanked them for their thoughtfulness, and they dropped me to the ground with a gentle thud.

The crowd cheered as we were led away to the principal's office, where the fight of the century was about to be fought, the fight to avoid being kicked out of school.

(Postscript: I received two weeks suspension. Whew!)

MR. & MRS. MONTERA

"I hate you," she shrieked, over and over again, loud enough for the entire neighborhood to hear, not caring what others might think of her total lack of control. And listen they did to the ongoing soap opera that Mr. and Mrs. Montera played out for them daily. He would never make a fool of her again. "Never!"

Dismissing her with a shrug of shoulders, he smirked and walked out the door, leaving her standing there alone in total disbelief. He had done the unthinkable this time. He had cheated on her with her best friend. Privately, she knew of his philandering, but now she would be held up to ridicule, knowing her former best friend was also a blabbermouth.

"Not this time, Señor Montera," she shouted, letting everyone know the subject of her wrath.

Blinded by rage, she ran after him, down the stairs and out of the building. It didn't matter that she was dressed in a flimsy negligee that exposed her nipples and every curve she had proudly saved for his eyes only. He was not going to get away so easily this time by just walking away.

Hearing the start of the engine, she ran to his car, threw open the door, climbed in and attacked him with all the passion within her, calling him names that even she did not know the meaning of. As her tears subsided and her vision cleared, she discovered she was in the wrong car and had been screaming at a total stranger, who did nothing other than stain his pants.

"Oh, excuse me," she mumbled, as she gingerly climbed out of the car and crawled back into her apartment, hoping she would disappear by just turning off the lights.

SILENCE IS GOLDEN

Cookie mumbled from the last pew as she waited for her grandmother to emerge from the confessional. "For someone so holy, she sure has a lot to confess."

Cookie had already made her confession, said her Hail Mary's and now sat fidgeting with a pamphlet about St. Anthony. "I'm glad I don't have as many sins as she does. Besides, all Father Wilson ever wants to hear about is sex."

Every week since she could remember, Father Wilson would pry her with sexual questions and become clearly annoyed when she had no specific answers.

"Has a boy ever touched you there? Have you ever touched yourself?"

"What kind of crazy questions were those?" She would find herself blushing. "Why would I want to do that?"

"You must remember that a priest is still a man," her grandmother advised her on their walk home. "Every man has sex on his mind, even priests. Sex is dirty, and you should never do something dirty."

"Gee, Grandma, if it's so awful, how come you had thirteen children?"

Her grandmother's eyes shut as she grabbed Cookie's blouse and marched her back to church and led her to the head of the line of sinners.

"You go back in there, Señorita, and tell the Father that you have been fresh to your *abuelita*."

The last thing she heard before reentering the confessional was the cluck-clucking of the holy ones, who all agreed she should be damned to hell.

SUNDAY, FEBRUARY 10TH, 1974

Lincoln Hospital was singing that day. Not the patients who sat waiting in the emergency room. They weren't singing. They sat in pain or discomfort waiting to be called. But everybody else was singing. They were singing in Spanish because most of the people working there that day were Latinos. Maybe they were singing because it was Sunday. Who knows why people sing?

It had been years since I had been to Lincoln Hospital. I had moved away from the South Bronx quite a few years back. I had almost forgotten what the emergency room was like. It was still dirty. It was still crowded. The only difference was that everybody was singing.

I was there to identify the body of my father, who had died of a heart attack on his way to work that morning. He always worked on Sunday. I knew he had died because two policemen brought me the news.

I walked over to a singing attendant standing behind the front desk and asked about my father. He asked for my name and, after looking through a few papers, stopped singing. In fact, he became downright solemn. He didn't know that I knew my father was dead and sent me into another room where I was to speak to a doctor. The room was more of a hallway behind two doors. There were patients in wheelchairs or lying on gurneys waiting to be attended to. Two Latino policemen, one tall, one short, stood in that room. They began to flirt with me while they kept singing.

I stood there and listened to them sing and watched them flirt, wondering what they would do if they knew what I was there for. After a while, a black nurse asked me who I was and what I wanted. I told her, and she immediately went and found the doctor who had examined my father. Neither she nor the doctor knew that I knew he was dead.

Both of them took me into a little room, asked me to sit down and then explained to me about my father. I told them I knew he had died and that I was there to identify him. They asked me to wait until they could find someone to take me to the morgue. They both left and I waited.

After a while, the doctor returned and told me they couldn't find anyone to take me there because everyone was out to lunch. He escorted me into the hallway and asked to wait again. I did. A black male attendant came through the room carrying a portable radio and he sang along with it. The two policemen kept singing.

I waited and waited, listening to the music. I stared at the patients on the gurneys and wheelchairs, wondering what was wrong with them as they stared at me leaning against a wall, wondering what was wrong with me. After about a half hour, I asked the doctor if he had yet found someone to escort me to the morgue.

He had forgotten about me. He asked around and found that the morgue was closed for lunch. "Come back in an hour."

What does a person do in Lincoln Hospital for an hour? You could break down crying because you know your father is dead. That's what I wanted to do. Not there, though. Not in that God-forsaken place.

I looked around for a bathroom and found one. It was filthy, and there was no toilet paper. I walked all over that hospital looking for a bathroom that had paper. That was as good a way to spend the time as any. I passed an orderly who was singing while carrying a tray of food from the cafeteria. I wondered how he had the stomach to eat in a place like that, but that was his business. The smell of the food made me want to vomit, but I didn't.

I walked to the other side of the hospital and found a room where I could smoke. I sat down and waited and smoked cigarette after cigarette. I was in the main waiting room and I watched the two black women behind the desk going about their business. A Latina girl walked over to them to inquire about a patient. They couldn't understand Spanish, and she couldn't understand English. I thought of going over and translating for them but instead I just watched them as the black women tried to *explaino* in *Spanisho* that there was no such person listed in the hospital. I wondered if they had lost him.

I noticed that the majority of the nurses that passed through the room were Asian. I noticed the doctors all seemed to come from the Middle East. I wondered how in hell everyone communicated with each other since most of the patients seemed to be Spanish speakers. I noticed that my hour was almost up and I walked back through the halls, passing by the cafeteria again, and again almost vomited, until I reached the emergency room.

Once back inside, the singing policemen could no longer hold back their curiosity.

They asked what I was doing there. I told them and they stopped singing. They stopped singing and they stopped flirting.

I found the doctor again, who then asked one of the two policemen to escort me to the morgue. One of them walked me a few feet away to two doors that led outside the building. Once outside, he pointed to a door and told me that was it. Then he left.

I walked through that door and found my aunt inside, waiting for me. She had gotten worried and come down to the hospital to help me out, just in case. She asked where I had been, and I told her that I was on the other side of the hospital. There was a man there who had come to take my father's body to Bellevue Hospital, and I had almost missed him. He asked us if we wanted to see the body, and we said yes.

We walked into this small room filled with drawers. He pulled out one of the drawers, and there was my father. There was no time to breathe before the drawer was opened and pulled out. He opened it as quickly and efficiently as a secretary opens a file drawer. I looked at my father lying in that drawer: he seemed to be sleeping. He looked as he always looked, dressed in his work clothes with his hair messed up, as it always was when he came home from work. There was only one difference. One bare foot had a tag tied to it. The other foot still had his shoe on.

I looked away from the tag in time to see a fat man in an adjoining room stuffing his face with a bowl of rice. I couldn't believe it. There sat a man eating a bowl of rice right in the next room, while my father lay dead in a file drawer.

The attendant closed the drawer and told us that we would have to go to Bellevue Hospital later on to identify my father again. They had to take him to the coroner's office there. He asked us to give him time to get the body down there before we went. Why did we have to identify him twice? It was the law.

I asked about my father's belongings. He told me to ask the other morgue attendant about them, and that man told us that his belongings were in the property office. We asked where it was, and after of bit of hesitation, he agreed to show us. He was a black man and walked slowly. I wanted to get out of that hospital so badly, and he walked so slowly.

I found myself becoming angry. We walked back through the emergency room again. The staff was still singing. I kept wanting him to walk faster. I thought of Stepin Fetchit, the black film actor, and almost laughed. It was easier to control my anger by pretending to be following Stepin Fetchit to the property office. We walked past the cafeteria until we were at the other side of the hospital. There, we were finally at the property office where we were to ask about my father's belongings. Although there were people inside the office, the "property office" was closed because it was Sunday. I wondered how they put his belongings there? It had to be open when they put them there, but it was closed to get them out. We would have to come back on Monday.

We left the hospital, and I breathed in the air, which seemed cleaner than any air I had ever breathed before. I walked towards the car and thought about the tag on my father's toe and the man with the bowl of rice and the singing attendants and policemen and Stepin Fetchit and I wanted so badly to cry. I wanted to cry, but I still had to go to Bellevue to identify my father.

THE CHANGE

Doctor Liebowitz made his way down Longwood Avenue toward Southern Boulevard. He had done this every weekday morning since he opened his practice over twenty-five years ago. He walked past Tommy's Bodega trying to remember what it was before Tommy took it over. He did remember that directly across the street used to be the drugstore and beyond that Sheinman's shoe store which now sold Latino records but kept its sign. The whole neighborhood had changed from Jewish to Latino in what seemed to him an instant. He was one of the last Jews who still worked there and he felt kind of proud of that fact. Besides, there was always room for a doctor, no matter what neighborhood you inhabited. Sick people were sick people, no matter where they lived.

He passed the same ragtag group of boys that he did every day and every day he'd hear the same taunts from them. Taunts that were juvenile and quite stupid to be frank.

"Doctor, help me. Give me something for my stomach. I can't stop farting."

And the inevitable "Help, I've fallen and I can't get up."

This brought roars of laughter from the others and eye rolling from the doctor. Over and again, he'd think to himself: "Whoever made up that commercial should be shot on sight."

He'd smile with the group of jokers, the same way he used to smile with the group of Jewish boys who joked with him years before.

"You got any of them little liver pills, Doc?"

He'd pray for something smart from any of them, but it never came. Kids were kids, no matter what their background was. There was, however, one kid that stood out from the rest. He alone bothered the doctor to no end, and the curious part was there was no reason why. They called him Pedro, and there was something about him that was different. He never spoke, but you knew he was the leader by the way they followed his every move. He was the one you didn't want to be on the wrong side of. He was nice enough looking, not too tall like a few of his cohorts or too short like the rest of them. His skin was a beautiful bronze color that stood out from most of them. The others looked weather-beaten, or too old for their ages, but he hadn't lost the country he came from yet.

Doctor Liebowitz knew he was the one to never make eye contact with and he never did. Always eyes down or straight ahead when he passed. It infuriated him and he wished it would stop. He hurried away towards his office. Once inside, he loosened his tie, unbuttoned his jacket and regained his composure. He checked his appointment book and wished he hadn't scheduled so many people for one day. He'd have to talk to Mrs. Handel about her pressure, knowing she was not taking her pills. He'd have to tell Mr. Torres to cut down on his drinking or else, but more than anything, he hated to have to tell Mrs. Fox that the lump on her breast was cancerous.

He heard rustling with keys at the door but made no effort to get up. It was his nurse. Margaret, and though early, she was still late to him. He watched her through the slit in the door as she made herself a cup of coffee and took exactly three cookies from her drawer, which was her breakfast every morning.

"Maybe she'll surprise me and take two or four someday" he thought, but it never happened. It was always three, and today it irritated him more than ever. Perhaps seeing Pedro had triggered this feeling or maybe he was just tired of the routine of everything and just needed a vacation. Maybe it was time to really think about retiring. He did think of it often but not often enough to chuck it all in. He rang for Margaret and watched as she spilled her coffee on the desk and floor, grabbed some paper towels and wiped it up.

"Jesus, Mary and Joseph," she muttered. "I wish he would tell me when he's here and not scare the bloomers off of me."

He rang again as she threw the dirty towels into the wastebasket.

"I'm coming. I'm coming" she repeated in a murderous tone that made him smile at his shenanigans. She picked up the appointment book and hurried into his office. He had sufficiently ruined her day, and it had just begun. Through teeth they said their good mornings, and it was off to the races before the first patient arrived.

One by one the patients filed in and out of the examination room, each one believing their story was the most important one he would hear and each one receiving the amount of understanding deemed sufficient by the doctor. There were times when his mind wandered but he caught it in time to bring it back to the present. One by one they filed in and out until the waiting room was empty and the last one had finally gone. He could hear Margaret counting out change for the bus like she always did. Then the same question every night floated through the intercom.

"Will there be anything else, Doctor?"

Margaret never waited for an answer. Her coat was on, and she was out the door. She had given herself five minutes to walk to the corner to catch the bus and she hadn't missed it in the five years she had worked for Dr. Liebowitz. He was glad she was gone, no pleasantries exchanged. He looked forward to unwrapping the peanut butter and jelly sandwich in his bag. Every day his wife made him the same sandwich and every day he ate it with gusto. He was easy to please, and had she switched it for something else, she knew his disappointment would have been unparalleled. She loved him for his easygoing ways and the way he would praise her dinners, even though she knew she was a lousy cook, let alone homemaker. That was the Liebowitz household, and she was proud to be a part of it.

✿ ✿

The ruckus outside of the door unnerved him, and before he could get to it, he watched as the doorknob turned. He prayed that Margaret didn't forget to lock it as she usually did or that she had come back for some unexplained reason. Instead, he heard Joni's voice loud and shrill as she opened the door and yelled inside.

"Dr. Liebowitz? Doctor, Doctor are you here? Where are you?"

His instincts told him to hide, not knowing why, but he knew Joni since she was born and the fear in her voice was not to be ignored.

"What's wrong, Joni?"

His answer came behind her in the form of Pedro, his hand cradled by a towel filled with blood.

"You have to help him, Dr. Liebowitz. He'll bleed to death."

"Calm down, Joni. Let me have a look at it."

"Show him, Pedro."

Pedro began to unwrap the bandaged hand.

"My God, there's glass in there."

A large shard of glass protruded from his wrist.

"He has to go to emergency."

"No, doctor. He won't go."

"Why not? He'll bleed to death." Turning to Pedro, "Do you understand me? You have to go to Emergency right away."

The boy began to wrap his hand again.

Dr. Liebowitz turned to Joni. "Can he understand me? What's the matter with you? They can help him."

"He's illegal. They'll send him back. He can't go back."

"My God, he'll die without help."

"You help me."

This was the first time he had heard Pedro speak. He had assumed that the boy had a gruff voice and spoke like a man, tough and strong. Instead, the voice was soft, not intimidating at all. But it was his eyes that said it all. This was no average youngster like the other kids in the neighborhood. He had the eyes of someone who shook hands with death more than once, and the reason behind it did not matter.

"Help him, please."

Dr. Liebowitz looked at the little girl who used to belt out songs on Ellman's countertop in his candy store while everyone cheered and asked for song after song. He remembered how beautiful she was as a child, graceful with the world at her feet. Everyone in the neighborhood loved this talented child who would sing her heart out every chance she got. What was she doing with this "gangster," for want of a better word. Was the Belle of the Ball now being used by this killer to stay alive?

"My mother will pay you," she cried, unable to hold back her tears any longer.

"I know that, Joni. Help me get him into the examination room."

He knew in his heart that this would be the last patient he'd ever see.